Gil's ALL FRIGHT Diner

Gil's ALL FRIGHT Diner

A. LEE MARTINEZ

TOR®

A TOM DOHERTY ASSOCIATES BOOK
NEW YORK

GIL'S ALL FRIGHT DINER

Title lettering by Iskra Johnson
Spot art by Jeff Soto

A Tor Book
Published by Tom Doherty Associates, LLC
175 Fifth Avenue
New York, NY 10010

www.tor.com

Tor® is a registered trademark of Tom Doherty
Associates, LLC.

Library of Congress Cataloging-in-Publication Data

Martinez, A. Lee.
    Gil's All Fright Diner / A. Lee Martinez.—1st ed.
        p. cm.
    "A Tom Doherty Associates book."
    ISBN-13: 978-0765-31143-6 (hardcover)
    ISBN-10: 0-765-31143-7 (hardcover)
    ISBN-13: 978-0765-31471-0 (trade paperback)
    ISBN-10: 0-765-31471-1 (trade paperback)
    1. Zombies—Fiction. 2. Vampires—Fiction. 3. Werewolves—Fiction.
4. Restaurateurs—Fiction. 5. Diners (Restaurants)—Fiction. I. Title.

PS3613.A78638G55 2005
813'.6—dc22
                                                        2004063791

First Edition: May 2005

Printed in the United States of America

0   9   8   7   6   5   4   3   2   1

This book is dedicated to the following people in order of importance:

To Me, because I wrote it.

To Mom, without whom I probably wouldn't have.

To the men and women of the DFW Writer's Workshop. Their wise advice made this book better, although I'll later deny I ever said anything of the sort and claim this part of the dedication is a typo.

And to Don "The Dragon" Wilson.

Gil's All Fright Diner

ONE

In the middle of nowhere, along a quiet stretch of road, the diner dreamt of the hungry dead. And of two men.

Well, not men exactly.

Earl bounced in his seat as the pickup quaked. His beer slipped and settled in his lap. He grunted curses as he snatched up the can too late to prevent a yellow puddle around his groin.

"Hell, Duke, do you gotta hit every goddamn hole in the road?"

Duke shrugged and offered a mumbled apology.

"Yeah, well just try and watch it."

Earl reached into the pool of empty beers. "Damn it, Duke! If that's the last beer, I'm going to have to kick your ass." Like Arthur with Excalibur, he withdrew a full beer. "You got lucky." He popped it open and gulped down half its contents.

Duke grunted.

"How we doing on gas?" asked Earl.

"We got enough."

"How much we got?"

"Enough."

"Damn it, Duke, can't you just answer a goddamn question?"

Duke took a moment to lean out his window and spit. "We got enough, Earl."

The rusty gray truck bounced down the dusty road, more of a dirt trail really. Worn shocks were helpless against the rocky, hole-ridden roadway, and with each jolt, the engine rattled as if it might rip free. The tape player didn't work; something the passengers had learned at the cost of a Hank Williams, Jr. cassette. Spools of black tape hung from the radio's jaws, the inevitable end of an unsuccessful rescue attempt. The passengers rode in silence with only the clatter of seventy-six empty beer cans to fill the quiet. Seventy-six was the exact number of tallboys that could fit in the front seat before space limitations demanded a transfer to the bed.

The vehicle was an unlikely means of transport for the Earl of Vampires and the Duke of Werewolves. But for a vampire who happened to be named Earl and a werewolf who liked to be called Duke, it was perfectly acceptable. Truth be told, they had called on much worse when the occasion demanded it.

"We got like thirty more miles to the nearest station, y'know?" Earl glanced at the fuel gauge. It trembled on empty. "Shit. Should'a filled up at the last place. I told'ja, didn't I?"

He contented himself by tossing dirty looks Duke's way the next few minutes.

The vampire was a stringy fellow, pale—as one would expect—with an overbite, a large nose, and a ridiculously unsuccessful comb-over. The werewolf was large and hairy, even in his current man form. His monstrous gut barely managed to squeeze behind the steering wheel. A green baseball cap tried, and failed miserably, to contain the thick mane of dark brown hair atop his head. He had never been able to grow a beard, but a permanent five o'clock shadow covered his face.

Earl wore threadbare overalls that were at least as old as he was. (Which, for the record, was much older than he looked, but still not all that old for a vampire.) Duke wore denim jeans, a leather jacket, and a T-shirt emblazoned with the slogan NO FAT CHICKS.

"Next chance we get, Duke, we should get some new tires, too."

"Tires are fine."

"This one's ready to blow."

"No it ain't."

"What the fuck to do you know about tires, dipshit?"

"I know it ain't going to blow."

"Fine, but when it does, you're changing it."

"Fine."

Duke didn't bother to point out the truck was currently riding on its spare.

Rattling quiet fell on the cab once again. It lasted through the next half-hour. The pickup's working headlight cut through the darkness of a cloudy night and sliver of a moon. The occasional forlorn mailbox or animal carcass marked the otherwise unremarkable miles. Finally, a beacon of shimmering neon dared pierce the dark. It was a ten-foot sign beside a bunker of concrete. The sign read GIL'S ALL NIGHT DINER.

Duke pulled off. "I'm hungry," he explained, before Earl could set about busting his balls.

Earl set about to busting anyway. "You could'a ate earlier. I told'ja to get something earlier."

"Wasn't hungry then." Duke tugged the brim of his cap so that it nearly covered his eyes as he pulled his girth free of the driver's seat. The pickup's suspension groaned as the truck rose three inches.

"You could'a got a sandwich. That's your problem. You never think ahead. You're always living in the now. You've got one of them there reactive minds."

Duke cursed the day Earl had gotten his hands on a dog-eared copy of *Dianetics*.

The werewolf stopped to sniff the air.

"Now what?" Earl asked.

"Nuthin'." He tilted his head. "Thought I smelt sumthin' for a minute there."

"What? What d'ja think you smell?"

"Zombies."

"Jeezus, Duke, there ain't nuthin' for a hundred miles. Where the hell would zombies come from?"

"Over there."

Duke jerked his thumb over his shoulder as he entered the diner. As if on cue, the dust raised by the pickup's arrival settled, revealing a small cemetery.

"Oh."

Duke went inside.

A big black raven perched atop the diner's neon sign. The bird tilted its head to stare at Earl with one cruel ebony eye.

"What are you looking at?"

He flung a pebble at the raven, but missed. The bird didn't seem to care. It stayed on its perch without ruffling a feather. Sighing, Earl headed inside.

Duke's worn hiking boots squeaked with each step across the diner's worn linoleum floor. Earl's flip-flops mutely thumped. The diner was abnormally large given its desolate location. There were enough booths, tables, and barstools to service a small army. But the room was empty. The overhead lights hummed obnoxiously. Two cheap desert landscapes hung by the bathrooms. A potted fern hung from a support column. A cracked ceramic pot sat in a corner. These efforts failed miserably to add character, and the place was so devoid as to be almost vulgar in its blandness.

The most eye-catching detail was a brownish red stain, about a foot long at its widest, at the base of the column. A normal person wouldn't give it much thought, mistaking it for rust or mildew. But both Earl and Duke had sensitive noses. It smelled of blood. The stain looked old, but the odor, though subtle, was fresh.

A voice came from the back. "Be right with you."

They found seats at the counter. The odor of grease made Duke's stomach rumble.

Earl continued with his psychoanalysis. "Now me, I've got goals, and my mind acts upon those goals in an enlightened manner. I've achieved myself a state of clear. Whereas you just act on whatever impulse enters that fool head of yours."

"Least I got myself a shadow."

The vampire glanced at the floor. His shadow was indeed gone again. It did that quite often. Sometimes disappearing for hours or even days. Earl always hated that. He just knew that wherever it went, it was having a better time than him. And when it was in its rightful place, it had a tendency to move around against his will, taunting him and making a general nuisance of itself. Of all the problems of the undead (too many to list, really) the shadow was perhaps the most trivial, yet the most annoying.

Knowing how much it bothered Earl, Duke cracked a hint of a smile.

Earl scoured his mind for a clever comeback. He finally settled for a snarled, "Fuck you."

The kitchen doors swung open, and a tall, plump woman lurched into the front. She wore a T-shirt and jean cutoffs that hugged her jiggling behind, but only barely. Cellulite rolled down her legs in flapping waves with each step. A soiled apron stretched across her immense breasts. Her hair, a frazzled bleached-blonde mess, slung to the left of her face and just past her shoulders. She smiled, revealing teeth the size and color of corn kernels. A stained tag pinned to her collar had the name Loretta in bright green letters next to a beaming happy face.

"Morning, boys. What can I get you?"

Duke fished deep into his pockets and dropped a handful of crumpled bills and eighty-three cents in change. "What'll that get me?"

The waitress pushed the money around with the eraser end of her pencil. "Grilled cheese sandwich, some fries, cuppa chili, and a Coke."

He nodded.

"Nuthin' for me, thanks," Earl piped in. "I already ate."

Loretta disappeared into the back. Duke, who had seen a

man's fresh innards spilt upon the ground on more than one occasion, averted his eyes from the disagreeable trembling flesh of her exit. Earl was too busy looking for his shadow to notice.

The waitress's head bobbed about in the rectangular window that allowed a glimpse into the kitchen. "Where you boys headed?"

"Nowhere in particular," Earl replied. "Just driving."

"Nuthin' wrong with that. Hell, sometimes I wish I could pull up stakes and just go wherever the Good Lord sees fit to take me." She slapped something on the grill, and sizzling filled the air. "You boys didn't see nuthin' strange on your way in, did'ja?"

Earl snorted. "Strange like what?"

"Nuthin'. You'd know it if you saw it. So where you from?"

"Around."

She grinned. "Sorry, I just get to chatting on these slow nights. Don't mean to pry into your business."

Ten minutes later, she set a plate before Duke. The cheese dripped a puddle of grease, and the fries were soggy and brown. The chili was steaming hot, though. He dipped his spoon into the thick brown concoction and took a bite.

"How is it?" Earl asked.

"Good. Little heavy on the garlic."

Duke leaned close and let his traveling companion get a strong whiff of his breath. Earl recoiled, tumbling off his stool and hitting the floor. His nostrils flared, and his face contorted into a scowl.

"You asshole."

Duke chuckled.

Loretta smiled. Her smile vanished as her eyes fell on the glass diner doors. "Aw, damn it. Not tonight."

Earl glanced to the front. Nine shambling corpses in various stages of decay were pressed against the glass. Their yellow eyes (for those that had eyes) stared hungrily. Purple tongues licked peeling lips.

"Told'ja I smelt zombies," Duke said without turning from his meal.

The walking dead smashed their way through the glass doors. The lead corpse, in a blue paisley suit, stumped forward on stiff legs.

"Don't you worry none, boys. I'll handle this."

Loretta pulled a double-barreled shotgun from behind the counter, took aim, and squeezed the trigger. The blue-suited zombie's head exploded in a rain of dirt, bone, and maggots. The corpse took one more step before falling over. The next zombie suffered the exact same fate.

She removed the spent shells and fumbled around under the counter. "Damn. I'm out of ammo. Hold on. I got some more in the back." With a speed that belied her size, she rushed into the kitchen.

The seven remaining zombies shuffled forward, slowly closing the fifteen feet from the door to the customers.

"You wanna handle this, Duke?"

"I'm eating."

"You saying I'm afraid?"

Duke sighed. For an enlightened vampire, Earl could be damned sensitive.

"I didn't say nuthin' of the sort."

"You implied it."

"Damn it, Earl. If I got sumthin' to say, I just say it. I don't imply shit." The werewolf swallowed a third of his sandwich in one bite. "Anyhow, don't you got one of them clear minds. I didn't think you got scared."

"I'll show you who's scared."

The vampire rolled up his sleeves and walked up to a zombie. He unleashed a clumsy right hook. His target made no effort to get out of the way. The zombie's jawbone flew across the room with a dry crack. He stumbled back.

"I ain't scared of nuthin'."

He landed another punch on a second opponent. Her head spun around to face her back.

"I'm immortal, you dipshit!" Earl shouted to Duke. "You think a bunch of worm-ridden pricks are gonna bother me?"

He summoned all his unnatural strength and thrust his fist into a zombie's chest. Fragile ribs and desiccated organs gave way, and his forearm thrust through the corpse. He pulled, but the arm was stuck.

"Goddamn."

The impaled zombie grabbed him by the throat. Vampires didn't need to breathe, but even the undead could be inconvenienced by a crushed larynx. Earl kicked one of his attacker's thin legs. The limb broke off at the knee. The hopping zombie tightened its grip as its brothers and sisters encircled their prey.

"Uh, Duke," Earl rasped, "A little help here."

The corpses fell upon him in a hog pile.

"Shit."

Duke stuffed a handful of soggy fries into his mouth and took off his jacket, followed by his T-shirt. He was in the middle of unlacing his boots when Loretta returned. "Where's your friend?"

He nodded toward the mound of moaning dead.

She blasted two of the corpses on top and reloaded hastily. "I'm really sorry about your friend there. How about a free slice of apple pie? Just let me take care of these godless abominations first."

Duke pulled off his jeans and stood completely naked. The werewolf found it saved time not to bother wearing underwear. He tossed his clothes in a heap on the counter.

"That's alright. I got it."

The bear of a man transformed into a wolf of a man. His impressive six-foot-five frame expanded and widened into a hairy ape-like shape. Powerful muscles bulged beneath coal black fur. Terrible claws sprouted from his fingertips. Thick yellow teeth grew from his gums. Duke dropped to all fours.

"Damnation," Loretta uttered breathlessly.

Your average zombie is not a combat machine. Their fighting prowess springs from a single-minded determination and a certain walking corpse stick-to-itiveness. Your average werewolf is an unrivaled killing machine, vicious teeth and claws coupled with supernatural grace, power, and the ultimate predatory instincts. Duke was not your average werewolf. He cut a swath through the corpses, twisting off their heads with casual effort. Within four seconds, the five remaining corpses were sprawled on the floor in a twitching mass.

"Damn it, Duke," Earl growled. "I think one of those things took a bite out of me."

Duke chuckled dryly. "Zombies ain't got no stomach for undead flesh. You know that." He walked back to the counter and had a seat. The metal stool bent under his full lycanthrope weight.

"Now, how 'bout some of that pie?"

Loretta eased back the shotgun's hammers. "You boys ain't planning on any funny business?"

"That depends on the pie."

"Actually, ma'am, we ain't killed nobody in ages," Earl reassured her.

"What about that trucker last Tuesday?" Duke asked.

"Oh hell, he don't count. He was asking for it. Look, miss, under all that hair, Duke is just a big ol' puppy dog, and I already ate. What say you lower that. We won't hurt you, and unless you got silver buckshot in there, it won't really do much to either of us."

Loretta, seeing the wisdom of his words, laid her shotgun on the counter. "Well, you fellas seem nice enough, and you did save me some ammunition. Guess a free slice of pie ain't too much to ask in return."

She went to the rotating pastry display, currently empty save for half an apple pie.

"This sort of thing happen much around here?" Earl asked.

She sighed. "Every couple of weeks. It's usually only three or four of the bastards. I don't have to tell you, it's really cut into my business."

"You tried anything about it yet?"

"Got the preacher to bless and exorcise the cemetery after the second time. I guess it didn't take. After that, I figured I could wait them out. That's the weird part. Can't be more than a hundred graves in that place, but I've killed more than a hundred and fifty since. Hundred and eighty-one counting that batch. Damned if I can reckon where they're all coming from. Nobody's been buried in there for years."

"Sounds like a problem," Earl remarked.

She nodded, setting a plate before Duke.

The werewolf wrapped his immense hands around a fork and took an experimental bite.

"Well?"

She stared at his wolf's head, looking for any sign of a smile on his muzzle.

"He likes it." Earl pointed to the werewolf's briskly wagging tail.

"Glad to hear it. I made it myself."

She clapped her meaty hands together. "Say, you fellas looking for work?"

"We can look into that zombie problem for you," Earl agreed.

"Actually, I was talking about helping me lay a new gas line for my stove. But if you take care of those damn corpses, I'd throw in a hundred bucks and some gas."

The werewolf and the vampire exchanged thoughtful glances.

Duke slid his empty plate toward her. "Throw in another piece, and you got yourself a deal."

TWO

Her name (or the name her adopted parents had given her) was Tammy, but her followers called her Mistress Lilith, Queen of Night. At the moment, she had only one disciple, and he was more interested in getting in her pants than aiding her in opening the way for the old gods. Chad Roberts was lacking in true devotion, but assembling a legion of believers in a dust bowl like Rockwood—five square miles of town spread across thirty—was no easy task. Chad wasn't her first choice, but he could be useful in a muscle-bound lackey sort of way.

Tammy and her cult of one squatted by the ceremonial fire in the burnt-out remains of Make Out Barn. He hummed the theme to *Bonanza* while tracing patterns in the dirt with his fingers. The firelight glinted off her ritual dagger.

"Uh . . . Tammy . . ."

She tossed him a hard look.

"Mistress Lilith," he quickly corrected, "I don't think they're coming."

Sighing, Tammy snatched up her worn copy of the abridged *Necronomicon* next to her pile of clothes. She flipped through the pages to the ritual of Thanatos's Risen Children, but there was nothing in the book to help her. They'd performed the ceremony a dozen times. Even Chad, who didn't have much in the way of brainpower and understood nothing of black magic, could execute the spell by memory. No, it wasn't a flaw in the casting. It had to be the zombies. They just weren't enough.

"Damn that fat old bitch."

Any normal person would flee from the risen dead. Why didn't she? Something new was needed. Something more powerful.

She leafed through the book, ignoring Chad's unblinking stare at her breasts. Tammy was used to the stares. Not just from her follower, but from all the boys (all nine of them her age) in Rockwood. She was far prettier than all the other girls. Except for Denise Calhoun, that fat cow with her C-cup boobs. But Denise was white trash whereas Tammy was adopted and the only Japanese girl in town, possessing an exotic edge over Denise, whose parents let her wear makeup, even though it made her look like a big slut.

"What do we do now, Mistress Lilith?" Chad asked, as he leaned closer and brushed her long, silky hair.

She shoved him away. "I'm thinking, dumbass."

Chad was not so easily discouraged. He flexed his overdeveloped pectoral muscles like some primate mating signal.

She kept reading.

"Are we going to do it or not?"

"Why don't you go into the corner and do it yourself?"

He stood, slouching. "Aw, come on, Tammy. Big Jimmy needs his lovin'."

"Mistress Lilith," she replied.

"Uh, sorry." He adopted a whiny tone. "Come on, Mistress Lilith. Please?"

"Oh, alright." She laid the book aside with a sigh. The jerk was impossible to ignore when he was horny—and he was always horny.

Chad grinned, grabbing a condom from his neatly folded trousers. Nineteen groaning, sweaty seconds later, Tammy climbed off Big Jimmy (all three inches of him), Chad fell dead asleep, and she returned to her research.

There was much to be done. Soon the planets would align. The Gate would open and flood the world with beautiful darkness. Her masters would ascend to their rightful thrones, and she would reign by their sides while Denise Calhoun screamed herself hoarse in eternal agony.

If she could only get inside that diner.

THREE

Loretta pulled the chain, and a dusty forty-watt bulb did its best to illuminate the diner's storeroom.

"It ain't much, boys, but it's the best in town. There's a Motel 6 a little ways up the road . . ."

"This'll do."

Earl entered, carrying one end of a steamer trunk. Duke, bearing his own end, followed. The werewolf dropped his side and the trunk struck the floor with a faint crack, raising a cloud of dust.

"Damn it, Duke. How many times I gotta tell you to be careful with this?"

Loretta swung her meaty arms around to denote the storeroom's amenities. "Got yourself a sink right there and a cot here. And there's some blankets and a pillow on that shelf under the canned corned beef. The sink can make a racket and don't drink the water if it's dark brown. Light brown's okay."

She paused to rearrange the shelves.

"Now I only got one rule in this room: no eating. It's hard enough to keep rodents out of here without leaving crumbs. And what with the zombies and all, I'm having enough trouble keeping my license."

"No problem." Earl threw open the trunk and climbed inside. "You wanna hand me that pillow, Duke?"

"What's wrong with the one you got in there?"

"It's flat."

"So what am I supposed to do?"

"Just give me the pillow, you prick. It's bad enough I gotta sleep in this damn box without having to deal with your shit."

Duke hurled the smudged pillow into the trunk. "Take it already."

"Thanks, hairball."

"You're welcome, Bela."

"One more thing I better make perfectly clear," said Loretta. "I don't know what sort of heathen acts you boys perpetrate in your spare time. That's your business. But I won't have anything indecent under this roof. That means no fornicating, no drinking, no smoking, and if you've got any special needs that you think I'd better not know about . . ." She focused on the vampire. ". . . take care of them elsewhere. We understand each other?"

"Yep." Earl shut his bed.

Morning came to Rockwood. Duke was nocturnal by nature. Loretta, as owner/operator of Gil's All Night Diner, slept days as well. But the former zombies (now just plain rotting corpses) weren't about to clean themselves up. Duke loaded the bodies onto Loretta's pickup while she swept up the broken glass.

"Why is it," she asked, "that not one damned zombie can figure out how to work a door? Even the stupidest danged fool can push."

Duke tossed the last corpse onto the bed as a brown police car pulled into the diner's unpaved parking lot. A tall, lean man stepped into the hard morning light.

"Morning, Sheriff."

He tipped his Stetson to her. "Loretta. I thought I saw buzzards. Had another incident last night, did'ja?"

"Yep. Sheriff, this is Duke. He'll be staying awhile to help me put in a new gas line. Duke, this is Sheriff Marshall Kopp. He's the law in this county."

Kopp chuckled. "She makes it sound more important than it is. We got good people in this county. All the trouble comes from passers-through. Didn't catch your last name there, pardner."

Duke wiped his sweaty brow with the back of his hands. "Smith."

Kopp smiled skeptically. He stood tall as Duke, but his slender frame fell under the larger man's shadow. He pulled off his sunglasses and looked Duke square in the eye. "Well, Mr. Smith, you look like a decent, law-abiding fella. I don't think we'll have any problems."

"No, sir."

"Glad to hear it." He bent down to scoop up a zombie leg. "Phew! These things ripen real quick in this heat."

"Tell me about it," Loretta agreed. "You ain't going to report this, Marshall?"

He shrugged. "Don't see why I should. Just as long as you clean it up before the buzzards get hungry."

Two giant birds roosted on the diner's sign. Several more circled overhead, cawing impatiently.

"I'm taking them over to Red's right now."

"You do that. I don't suppose I could trouble you for something cold to drink?"

"Help yourself."

Sheriff Kopp grabbed a soda, got into his car, and disappeared down the long, dusty road. Duke and Loretta climbed into the truck and headed in the opposite direction. Duke passed the ride silently cataloguing the scenery. There wasn't much to see. Just a flat expanse of desert broken by cacti, tumbleweeds, fields of brown grass, and the occasional building. Rockwood had grown without a master plan, and it showed.

There were mobile homes and adobe constructions, ramshackle cabins and three-story manors. Some had white picket fences and concrete driveways. Others were surrounded by razor wire, with cows and chickens milling about in the front yard. The only common element was a lot of empty land between each. The citizens of Rockwood valued their personal space.

Finally, they pulled up alongside a wooden building. A sign over the door read RED'S TAXIDERMY AND MORTUARY.

A pair of pit bulls raged at their chains, announcing the truck's arrival. A wrinkled, old black man emerged from the cabin.

"Got another load for you, Red."

He glanced at the pile of bodies. "Whoo doggie, there's a lot this time."

"Nine of 'em," she confirmed.

"I'll get the wheelbarrow. Don't mind the girls, son. They're all bark. Just as long as you stay out of their reach."

Hands in his pockets, Duke stood inches from their snapping jaws.

It took three trips with the squeaky wheelbarrow to transfer the moldering body parts from the truck to the crematorium in the back of the building. When it was done, Loretta counted out a handful of bills.

"Usual rate?"

"Forty bucks a head."

"Damned things are costing me a fortune."

"I'm giving you the bulk discount," Red pointed out.

"I know, and I appreciate it. But every time this happens I end up shelling out a couple hundred for the disposal and glass repair. And business ain't exactly booming back at the diner. Sometimes I wonder if the Good Lord is testing me."

"It would explain a thing or two," Red agreed.

Duke squatted beside the slavering canines and stuck out his hand.

"Wouldn't do that," Red cautioned. "Less'n you want to lose a finger."

The dogs stopped, sniffed his hand, and began licking his palm. He scratched their muzzles and patted their necks.

"Damnedest thing I ever saw. Those bitches hate everyone. Even me. I gotta knock the spunk out of 'em with a stick when I feed 'em."

The dogs wriggled on the ground as Duke rubbed their bellies. "I got a way with animals."

FOUR

Duke kicked Earl's trunk.

The lid cracked open an inch. "Dusk already?"

"Yep."

The trunk slammed shut.

"Get your ass up, Earl."

Earl's muffled voice moaned, "Just ten more minutes."

Duke tried to open the trunk, but the lid held, locked from the inside. He beat on the steamer's side. It rattled with each blow.

"Damn it! Just ten more minutes!"

"Ten more minutes, my ass," Duke grumbled as he hefted the heavy trunk in the air. Even in his current man shape, he was twice as strong as most men his size, and there weren't many men his size. He turned the trunk upside down and shook.

"Alright already, you dipshit!"

Chuckling, Duke threw in three extra shakes before setting

it back down. The lid popped open, and the woozy vampire emerged.

"Jee-Zuss Kee-Rist, Duke, what's up your butt?"

"While you've been sleeping, I've been digging all afternoon." He slapped some of the dirt off his pants.

"Ain't my fault I got me a skin condition."

Duke frowned as he extended a full mason jar to Earl. The vampire set the red liquid under his big nose.

"What's this?"

"Breakfast. I had Loretta squeeze off some hamburger juice."

"Hell, Duke, you know I can't drink this cold stuff. Screws with my digestion something fierce."

"Suit yourself. Saw some livestock about a mile west."

"Livestock?"

"It's a small town, Earl. Probably be better if you watch what you eat." He turned on the faucet, which began to rattle and groan. He stuck his hands in the brown water and briskly rubbed them together.

"I can get a bite without causing any trouble."

"What about Tulsa?"

"You always gotta throw that in my face. I told'ja. That was an accident."

"Just keep to the cows and burros," Duke sighed. "Saw a llama ranch, too. They had some emus. Could give that a try if you're lookin' for sumthin' exotic."

"Fine. Can you at least come with me? Do that animal juju of yours."

Duke shook his hands dry. "Don't tell me you're afraid of a couple of cows."

"I ain't afraid of nuthin', you prick. It's just easier."

The werewolf laid on the cot and closed his eyes. "After breakfast, you better go and check that cemetery."

"Cemetery? By myself?"

"I'm doing the gas line. You're handling the zombies."

"But . . ."

Duke rolled to his side, his back to Earl. "Damn it, I'm tired here. Besides, you know you gotta better talent for that sort of thing."

"But . . . but . . ."

"Christ, Earl, you can be such a pussy."

The vampire straightened, scowling, his shoulders held back. "I ain't scared of nuthin'!"

"Yeah, yeah."

"Fuck you, Duke."

"Blow me, Earl."

Earl stormed from the diner, stopping just long enough to leave his breakfast by the kitchen stove. "Thanks, but I'll find my own."

Loretta cast a disapproving glance but didn't offer a reply. She hunched over a stubborn grease stain on the counter and continued scrubbing.

The vampire found his meal snoozing half-a-mile west of the diner. He leaned against the picket fence and watched the slumbering cow. Earl hated bovine blood. The only thing he hated more was cold bovine blood. He could live off the stuff, but that didn't mean he wanted to. But, much as he hated to admit it, Duke was right. This was safer.

Earl didn't need to kill his meal when he ate, but accidents happened. In a truckstop outside of Tulsa he'd been caught in the middle of dinner and nearly got his head lopped off by an eager bunch of religious nuts. Duke had saved his butt then and hadn't gone twenty-four hours without reminding him since.

He'd stalked livestock before and taken a bite of most domesticated animals. Emus he could stand, but they startled easy and kicked like a son of a bitch. Goat was good, but always left him hungry an hour later. Pig was almost pleasant, but he didn't like crawling in the mud. Horse had a horrible aftertaste, and donkey was terrible until properly aged. He'd never had llama. Never could get past all that hair to find a vein.

He hopped the fence and carefully snuck up on the cow. The beasts were easy pickings most of the time. Repressing a shudder, he remembered the time he mistook a bull for a heifer and found himself on the receiving end of a nasty goring that left an inconvenient hole in his intestines for the rest of that night and ruined a brand-new shirt. He double-checked for an udder before biting into the cow's jugular. He drank his fill (as much as he could stomach). The cow slept through the whole process.

He took his time walking back to the cemetery. Graveyards creeped him out. They always had. As a mortal, whenever he'd strolled past one, he could feel the eyes of the dead staring at him. He'd remind himself that there were no such thing as ghosts, no boogeymen or monsters. They were just figments of his imagination. Then he'd died and risen from the grave as one of the undead. Pushing monsters away into childhood fantasies was much harder after you'd become one. He'd discovered that most of the terrors that stalked the night weren't really terrors at all. They were mostly like regular folks, just trying to live their lives. As long as they were left alone they were perfectly harmless except for the occasional bite on the neck. Humans were the real terrors, always getting worked up and looking to kill something.

But cemeteries still creeped him out because ghosts creeped him out. And experience told him that every cemetery had at least one ghost in residence. Most people couldn't see them except as flitting shadows on a spooky night when the moonlight shined just right. As a vampire, Earl wasn't so lucky. He stood on that fine line between death and life, one foot on each side, though not truly belonging to either.

A waist-high wooden fence surrounded the two acres of neglected graveyard. The fence was barely standing in some places, completely fallen in others. A tall wrought-iron arch marked the entrance. The left gate clung to the arch by one rusty hinge. The right side creaked as it swayed back and forth. The plots on the other side were marked by homemade wooden headstones or the rare modest stone marker. Several tall cacti stood like unblinking watchmen. The wind picked up just long enough to raise a cloud of dust and bounce a tumbleweed across Earl's path.

"I ain't scared of nuthin'."

He walked through the gates.

Right away Earl saw something was wrong. Gaping holes covered the ground where zombies had dug their way out of their resting places. Earl counted sixty before losing interest. It looked as if not a single corpse had had the decency to stay in its grave. Except one.

It was near the back in a plot marked only by a sagging wooden cross. The cemetery guardian sat beside it. Earl could see the ghost plain as day. She looked as real and solid as any person of flesh and blood. There was little ghost-like about her, but he could tell. He could always tell. There was something about the pale, smooth consistency of ectoplasmic skin and the milky color of spectral eyes. The spirit wore cutoffs, a flannel shirt, and a pair of sneakers. Her long brown hair, tied in a ponytail, waved in the breeze. With dimpled cheeks, full blue lips, and a trim, athletic build, she was cute. But even a cute ghost was still a ghost and sent a shiver down Earl's spine.

He cleared his throat. "Pardon me, miss."

She looked up at him, then over her shoulder, then back at him. "Are you talking to me?"

"Don't see nobody else here."

"You can see me?"

He nodded.

"Really?"

"Yeah."

She got to her feet and waved her hands in his face. "Really?"

He grabbed her arms. "Really."

The ghost gasped and pulled away. "You touched me!"

If there was one thing he disliked more than ghosts, Earl decided, it was a ghost who didn't know how things worked.

She reached out and experimentally prodded him in the chest with her finger. When her hand didn't go through him, she smiled. "Seems like forever since I touched anyone. I almost forgot what it was like. Are you dead, too?"

"Undead," he corrected.

"Like a vampire? You're a vampire?" She looked the thin, gawky man up and down. "You?"

"We stopped wearing capes a while back. Name's Earl."

"I'm Cathy." She held out her hand for him to shake which he pretended not to notice. He didn't like touching ghosts if he could help it.

"Who's grave is this?" Earl asked.

"Mine."

"So you were the last person buried here."

"Yeah. How'd you know?"

"The last person buried in a graveyard usually stays behind to keep watch over it."

Cathy pounded her fist into her palm. "So that's it! Boy, is that a relief. I thought I was here because I had unfinished business or something."

"Didn't the last guardian tell you anything?"

"No. He just said, 'Adios, sucker,' and disappeared."

Shaking his head, Earl bent over to read Cathy's marker. There was no name, just the words "Rest in Peace" carved in the wood.

"I was just passing through when I got hit by a car. I didn't have any I.D. or family to look for me so they just buried me here. I guess they thought they were doing me a favor. So how long do I have to stay here?"

"Till the next body gets planted."

"But they don't bury anyone here anymore. That means I'm stuck here forever?"

"Might. Couldn't say for sure."

She frowned. "Great. Just great."

"Yeah. Sorry to be the one to tell you." He patted her shoulder in a halfhearted attempt at comforting. "So have you seen anything weird lately?"

"You mean, besides the zombies? Well, I did notice something odd. See that hole over there. A corpse crawled out of there yesterday, but there's no grave there." She pointed out a few more places where zombies had popped up without first being buried.

Earl considered the facts. Restless corpses might rise from their graves for a variety of reasons. Perhaps an ancient Indian curse or bad voodoo in the soil or any number of causes. But zombies did not spontaneously sprout like weeds. You had to have a corpse before you could have a zombie. It was the rules.

Unless someone was using black magic. Not just the everyday evil eye kind of black magic either. Something far more sinister, far more powerful, and far more dangerous.

This wasn't going to be as easy to fix as he had assumed.

Cathy followed him back to the cemetery gates. "You're leaving already?"

He tried to look into her eyes but couldn't do it. "I got some things I gotta take care of."

"Oh. Okay. Will I see you tomorrow?"

"I don't know. Maybe."

She smiled. "I'll keep an eye out for anything unusual. You should see me tomorrow."

"We'll see," he replied.

He briskly jogged back to the diner. He glanced over his shoulder one last time.

The ghost waved from across the street.

Earl waved back and ducked inside.

FIVE

Around nine o'clock, the diner received its first customers of the night. Four teenagers in a Volkswagen Beetle. They ordered the soup-and-salad special. While Loretta tossed their salad, Earl discussed the zombie problem with her.

"The way I see it, the problem can't just be with the cemetery like I first thought. See, your average zombie ain't all that bright. They just sort of wander about without someone telling them what to do. Now, so far, all these zombies have done is come into your place and hassle you. There ain't been any attacks on anyplace else?"

"Yeah, but mine is the closest," she reasoned.

"That's what I figured at first. Just a matter of location, but a'hundred-and-eighty-one zombies picking out this place just 'cuz it's the closest place don't add up when you think about it. That's just too many not to have a couple wander off some other direction. 'Less they're being directed."

Loretta sprinkled croutons on the wilted lettuce. "So somebody's doing this on purpose?"

"Maybe. 'Course, just because they're drawn to the diner that don't necessarily mean someone's telling 'em to. Just means there's some force behind it. It might not be a person at all."

She balanced the tray on one wide fat palm. "What else could it be?"

"Could be lots of things. Disembodied malevolent force like an angry spirit or an earthbound demon. Or the place might be a zombie magnet."

Scowling, she left the kitchen to serve her customers. She returned, scowling still.

"So what can I do about it? Should I get the preacher to exorcise the diner?"

"Couldn't hurt, but I don't think that'll change anything. Whatever you're dealing with is a lot more persistent than I'm used to seeing, what with it being able to conjure up zombies from scratch. Has anything strange ever happened before the corpse trouble?"

"Lotta strange things happen in Rockwood," she replied. "You'll have to be more specific. Strange like what?"

"I don't know. Anything involving the diner or the cemetery that don't seem right."

She slapped her flabby arms across her chest. "Gil Wilson, the last owner of the place, up and disappeared about five years back. Sheriff investigated and didn't find anything odd. Everyone pretty much assumed ol' Gil just got himself an impulse to wander and took off. He was a pretty odd fella. Never quite fit in.

"Anyway, the diner sat abandoned for three years. Finally, Marshall let me fix it up. It's still Gil's place technically, but nobody thinks he's coming back. Do you think his vanishing has sumthin' to do with all this?"

"Wouldn't rule it out just yet."

"And there's that splotch on the floor never goes away."

"It's blood," said Earl.

"Hell's bells, I already knew that. Can't clean up as much blood as I have without learning to spot it. Every time I get rid of it, it comes right back. Don't really know if it's related to all this, but it's a damn nuisance, just the same." She scratched her chins. "Can't think of nuthin' else right now. If you think it might help, I could ask around."

"Couldn't hurt."

Loretta left to check on her customers again. The storeroom door opened, and Duke emerged, his clothes wrinkled and his hair matted. He yawned, scratching his gut in the large region between his bellybutton and crotch.

"Evening, Duke."

Duke grunted. It was the closest he could come to conversation so soon after getting up. Grimacing, eyes half open, he fumbled noisily around the kitchen, slapping together a lopsided assemblage of bread, Spam, Swiss cheese, mayonnaise, and lettuce. He crammed it clumsily in his jaws and bit off a mouthful.

"Did you check out the cemetery?" he asked, wiping crumbs from his chin.

Earl nodded.

Duke popped open a Coke and took a long draught. He smacked his lips and took another bite.

"And?"

"I'm handling it, Duke."

"You talk to the guardian?"

Earl tossed Duke an annoyed glance. " 'Course I talked to the guardian."

"And?"

"And I'm handling it, you dipshit."

The kitchen door swung open. Loretta entered with two teenagers in tow. The boy was tall, athletic, with sandy blonde hair. The girl was a petite Asian in short shorts and a blue tank top.

Loretta performed quick introductions. "Boys, this is Chad and Tammy. These are the boys. They'll be helping me around the diner for a while."

Earl nodded in the teenagers' direction.

Duke packed the rest of his sandwich into his right cheek. Chewing, he took another drink of his soda before handing the half-empty bottle to Earl.

"I'm going back to bed."

"Nice meeting you," Tammy remarked as he shuffled back to the storeroom.

Duke murmured a reply as he departed.

Loretta dropped two hamburger patties on the grill. "Usuals, kids?"

"Yes, ma'am," Chad answered.

Tammy leaned against the counter. She stretched her arms over her head. Her tank top rose to reveal the lower curves of her bra.

Earl discreetly glanced at the ceiling.

"How long you planning on staying, sir?" She flashed a wicked grin. "If you don't mind me asking?"

"Couple of days."

She tossed her long black hair with her hands. Several strands fell across her shoulder. She sucked in a soft breath too light to be heard by mortal ears.

Earl's heart thudded in his chest. Or it would've had it ever thudded anymore. He felt the connection. Vampires had a supernatural sense to the carnal desires of humanity. She was attracted to him. Or, rather, the vampire in him. Not everyone could feel it. But when someone did, they couldn't help but be drawn to him. Guys wanted to be his best friend. Women wanted to jump his bones. Not that they ever really knew why. The attraction was almost always subconscious.

Tammy leaned over, giving him a good view of her cleavage. She traced her hands slowly up and down her tight, superbly proportioned thigh.

Earl was suddenly greatly appreciative of his loose overalls.

"I'll be eighteen in three months," Tammy threw out without prompting.

The comment hung awkwardly in the air alongside the stench of burning grease. Chad moved behind Tammy and looped his arms around her waist. Neither kid took their eyes off Earl.

The vampire smiled politely and nodded.

On the list of undead problems, he'd discovered the jailbait syndrome to be among the most bothersome. For whatever unfathomable reason, teenage girls were most prone to perceiving his undead nature. They were also the least capable of controlling their flood of raging hormones. The burden of self-control rested squarely on his shoulders. Most of the time, awkward teenage flirting made it easy to handle. Zits and braces didn't hurt either.

Tammy put a finger to her ruby lips and smiled.

There were exceptions.

Loretta came to his rescue. "Why don't you kids wait outside. This shouldn't take long."

"Sure, Miss Vernon," Chad replied, only too eager to drag his girlfriend from Earl's presence.

Against his will, Earl couldn't help but notice Tammy's perfectly round soon-to-be-eighteen butt. Her shapely calf was the last thing to disappear. Loretta cleared her throat in a manner that was equal parts disapproving and menacing. Earl decided it was a good time to retreat to the storeroom.

Chad wrapped his arms tightly around Tammy. His squirm-ing tongue probed her ear.

"Quit it, dumbass." She shoved her elbow into his side, and he pulled away. "Go to the other side."

"But, baby—"

She glared, and he gave in, sitting on the opposite side of the booth.

"I don't get it. Why would you want some skinny old guy when you could have this?" He flexed his overdeveloped biceps.

"He's a vampire," she sighed.

Entranced by the sight of his own impressive physique, Chad was only half-listening. "Who? The fat guy?"

"No, the skinny guy," she corrected. "The fat guy's a were-wolf."

"How can you tell?"

She considered explaining to him that, as a little girl, she'd discovered she possessed The Sight, the ability to see the supernatural world. The world most people spent their lives denying. Most people wouldn't notice Earl's lack of shadow or Duke's scarred palm. But they were obvious signs to someone who knew to look.

"Hey, baby," he asked, "is my right arm smaller than my left?"

"I don't know."

"I think it is." He glanced from arm to arm. "Goddamn it! I'll be right back, babe. I gotta go to the bathroom and check this out."

He got up and walked away, flapping his arms like a muscle-bound turkey. One day, Tammy consoled herself, she would have a better class of follower. In the meantime, he would have to do. Although, when the time finally came, she was greatly looking forward to sacrificing Chad to her gods. The thought of him strapped to an altar, begging for mercy, amused her for several satisfying minutes.

He returned, grinning like an idiot. "False alarm, babe."

She squinted at his arms. "Are you sure?"

A frown replaced his grin, and he stalked off to the bathroom once again.

Tammy chortled.

Her thoughts turned to the vampire and the werewolf. Their appearance was more than mere coincidence. Had the diner drawn them here? And if so, did they know its secret? And if they did, were they here to usurp her destiny? She'd worked too hard to allow a couple of outsiders to stop her now.

She would send down all the dark powers at her disposal to deal with these interlopers, if necessary. A mortal sacrifice was good. But a supernatural offering often bore more weight with the old gods. And two offerings were all the better. If it came down to that, she'd still sacrifice Chad, too. The old gods were always happy to snap up another soul. Even a soul as shallow and utterly worthless as his.

Besides, what was the point in ushering in a glorious new age if you couldn't have a little fun, too.

SIX

Morning approached, and Earl retired to his steamer as Duke reluctantly rose for another day's work. Earl fluffed up his pillow while Duke stretched the kinks out of his shoulders. Being men, their brief conversation turned to an inevitable subject: Tammy.

"She wanted me," Earl remarked. "Poor girl could barely hold herself back."

"Vampire thing?" Duke asked.

Earl glowered. "You saying a hot, young woman couldn't find me attractive if I weren't undead? You always gotta be knocking me down. I tell you what. I got laid plenty when I was still alive."

"Cousins don't count, Earl."

The vampire tossed his pillow in the trunk. "Up yours."

Duke chuckled. "Jeez, you can be such a sensitive puss. I was just funnin' you, Earl."

"Yeah, well those kind'a jokes ain't funny. Every time you

make 'em, you're reinforcing negative stereotypes. It's the sign of a reactive mind, y'know. People like you are the reason prejudice is still a problem."

"Give me a break, Earl."

"No. Really." Earl stepped into his trunk but didn't sit down. "You may think it's all harmless, just a little joke, but people like you are the foundation of intolerance. Without you, the dangerous bigots couldn't exist."

Duke closed his eyes and pinched the bridge of his nose. He'd heard this particular speech many times before. It was a hazard that came with an "enlightened" traveling companion.

"Okay. I'm sorry."

"I use'ta make jokes like that. I use'ta think they were harmless. But then I learned that they're products of a reactive mind."

"Alright, Earl. I got it. I got it. No more jokes. I'll just be a boring, preachy bastard all the Goddamn time."

"You just don't get it, do you?" Earl sighed.

"Guess not."

The vampire sat in his trunk and redirected the conversation back to its original topic. "She had a helluva ass."

"I didn't notice."

"You'd have to be blind not to notice."

Duke half-smiled. "Yeah. Guess so."

"Nice tits, too."

"Perfect legs."

"And those lips."

"Good neck," Duke added.

"What the hell is that supposed to mean?"

"Nuthin'. Just thought she had a good neck."

"Damn it. There you go again. Just 'cuz I'm a vampire you think I've got me a neck fetish. I'll take a good set of hooters over a great neck any day. I expect that sort'a stereotype from mortals, but you should know better, Duke. You've been watching too many movies. I mean, I like to eat, and I like getting laid. Just because I am what I am, that doesn't mean I like doing both at the same time." He screwed up his face in a queasy glower. "Just the thought makes me sick. Probably get a cramp or sumthin'."

Duke stomped over to the trunk, shoved Earl's head down, and slammed the lid shut.

"Go to sleep, Earl."

Duke had a quick cup of coffee to wake himself up, eager to get to work before the rising sun could bring the desert to a simmer. He also wanted to avoid the midday hours. Were-wolves were at their weakest, almost human, around noon. Even almost human, Duke was a formidable mountain of strength and endurance, but there wasn't much sense in making the job harder than need be.

He sipped his breakfast, studying his work so far. The ditch stretched twenty-five feet from the back of the diner's kitchen. There were twenty more feet to the propane tank. He could have dug the whole trench in one day, but he wasn't in a hurry. Earl would take a while to solve the zombie situation. He had plenty of time. He put aside his mug and picked up a rusty shovel.

A couple of hours later, Loretta appeared fresh from her morning nap. Her hair was pinned back in a sloppy bun. She wore jeans barely able to contain the voluminous mass of her hips, thighs, and butt. A flannel shirt, tied at her midriff, exposed her jiggling belly. The three top buttons were undone, allowing a healthy glimpse of her giant breasts. She carried a pitcher of lemonade in one hand, two glasses in the other, and a vaguely suggestive smile on lips thickly coated with bright red lipstick.

Duke put aside his shovel, wiped the sweat from his shirtless chest, and joined her in the shade offered by the diner.

"That's some good work there, Duke." She poured a tall glass and offered it to him.

"Thanks." He took a long drink. He didn't care all that much for lemonade, but he was thirsty enough not to care. "Almost ready to lay the pipe."

She nodded slowly. Her hair sagged further to the right.

He finished off his drink and crunched the ice.

Loretta fished a cube out of her glass. "Hotter than Hades today, ain't it?" She rubbed the ice across her double chin. Droplets ran down her thick neck.

"I've seen hotter."

"I just bet you have," she replied, batting her blue mascara eyelids.

Duke knew where this was heading, and it wasn't someplace he was real interested in going.

"My mamma always used'ta say that days like these were made for sinnin'." She ran the nearly melted cube across her bosoms. It slipped from her fingers and disappeared in the chasm between her immense breasts. "Damn it." She sent her hand in after it. While she fidgeted and shook in search of the lost ice cube, her left bosom came dangerously close to falling out of her shirt. Finally, when spillage seemed almost certain, the cube slid down her belly and landed in the dirt, where it melted instantly. She flashed an embarrassed grin before politely turning around to adjust her uneven breasts. She undid her bun and shook it out. Her chubby chins and the folds of her neck slapped together noisily. Her frazzled, blonde hair spread around her face like a pyramid of dried hay pinned to her head.

"It's been a while since the Good Lord has seen fit to bless me with a man to help around this place."

He avoided looking her in the eyes and instead focused on the dimple of a belly button in her rolling gut. He realized that might give her the wrong impression and glanced to the trench instead.

"You seem to be doing fine."

"I get by." She put her hands on her hips and stepped a little closer. "But there are some jobs only a man can handle."

Their eyes met. He may have been a werewolf, but she was the predator. Loretta wasn't an attractive woman, but she wasn't wholly repulsive. Underneath those many layers of flesh seemed a perfectly nice woman, and on several occasions, when he was drunk enough and horny enough, he'd accepted much worse offers. But he was stone sober today and only a little horny.

It seemed a raw deal. Earl got all the babes. Duke was lucky if he landed a two-hundred-pounder.

She placed a hand on his shoulder.

"You've worked up a good sweat here, haven't you? A man shouldn't be out in this kind of heat. I'd feel terrible if anything happened to you. Why don't you come inside for a while?"

Under the pretense of pouring himself another glass of lemonade, he delicately slid away. "Thanks, but I really want to finish the trench."

"You sure about that?"

"Yeah. If I get this done today, I can do all the pipe laying tomorrow. That way, you won't lose any business over it."

She sighed. "Well, it's your call, but if you change your mind, if it gets too hot for you, I'll be inside." Loretta redid her bun and returned to the diner.

Duke took measure of her quivering rear end. A six pack or two and the offer might start looking good. He swore off beer for a while.

A half-hour later, the diner's back door opened again. This time Red from Red's Taxidermy and Mortuary and a thin, older guy in jeans walked through it.

"Howdy, Duke." Red extended his hand. "Don't know if you remember me or not . . ."

Duke took Red's withered hand in a firm, but not too firm, shake. "Sure."

"This here is Walter Hastings."

Walter tipped his baseball cap. "Pleasure to make your acquaintance."

"Walter's been having some trouble with his cows, and I was just telling him about that trick you did with my dogs. How they're all nice and friendly now."

"I can make 'em mean again for you."

"No, that's alright. I like 'em better this way. But like I was saying, Walter's been having trouble with his cows, and I mentioned to him about your way with dogs. And he was wondering if maybe you had a way with cows, too?"

"You tried a vet?"

"Walter here don't trust vets. He thinks they're part of the . . . uh . . . what's that you're always saying there, Walt?"

"Inflated and excessive medical establishment."

"I guess I can take a look." Duke checked the burning sun hanging directly overhead. "I was about to take a break anyway."

"I surely would appreciate it. I'll pay you for your time. Say, twenty bucks?"

Duke stuck his shovel in the dirt. "Let's go."

Rather than squeeze in the cab of the pickup, he sat in the back along with Walter's dog, Betty. The mutt was a mix of two dozen breeds with notable traces of collie, Doberman, and, judging from her size, Saint Bernard. She laid her head on his lap, and Duke scratched behind her ears.

"Told'ja he had a way with animals," Red said.

The truck bounced down the road, pulling off after a few miles. The vehicle cut across Walter's land to a small herd of six thin cows. They were mostly skin and bones, their ribs showing through their sagging flesh and their deflated udders hanging limply. One lifted her head from the dry brush she was chewing to check out the approaching truck. She resumed grazing.

"So what exactly is the problem?" Duke asked as he hopped off the truck to take a look.

"Well, they aren't sick, and they're not eating any less, near as I can determine. They're just losing weight, and they stopped giving milk."

"Anything else?"

"They seem kind'a stupid." Walter pointed out a large

Jersey. "Melinda here use'ta be smart as a whip. For a cow. Now she's just got this—I don't know—empty look in her eyes. Like she don't even know me."

Duke circled Melinda twice. He ran his hand along her bumpy spine and checked her tongue and teeth. He patted the cow's thin neck. Melinda snorted dryly and stirred.

"I think I see your problem here."

"Nuthin' serious, I hope."

Duke pulled his pocket knife. " 'Fraid so. What you got here is six dead cows." He stuck the blade deep into Melinda's side between her ribs. The cow didn't seem to mind. He pulled out the knife and stuck his finger in the wound. "Yep. No blood, see? It's all dried up."

Walter and Red stepped in for a closer look.

"Son of a bitch," Red remarked.

Walter pulled off his cap and scratched his tangled gray hair. "Sweet Jesus, I ain't never seen nuthin' like that. So what are we talking about here? These cows are like zombies or sumthin'?"

Duke nodded. "Yep."

"Hell. I knew Loretta was having problems, but I didn't think cows could become zombies. How's sumthin' like that happen?"

"Couldn't say, but the whole lot will have to be put down. Right now they're still eating grass, but they'll be craving flesh soon."

"But they're dead. How do you kill them?"

"Bullet in the head should work, same as any zombie."

"The whole herd?"

"Sorry."

Walter patted Melinda between her eyes. "I'm gonna miss you, old girl. I got a thirty-eight in the glove box."

"That'll do."

"Uh . . . how long do we got before they get hungry?" Red asked.

"Not long, I'll bet," Duke replied.

"How about now?"

The other men saw that the herd had surrounded them unnoticed. The cowbells should've warned them, but none had been paying close enough attention.

"Damn," Duke swore under his breath. This sort of thing would happen now.

While the sun was up he was stuck in his man form. One almost human werewolf and two unarmed geezers weren't much of a match for six walking dead Jerseys.

Melinda raised her head and uttered a low, haunting howl. The rest of the herd joined her in a bloodcurdling moan that seemed to bubble up from the sulfurous pit of Hell itself.

"Mo-o-o-o-o-o-o-o-o-o-oo."

Eyes full of unnatural hunger, loose lips smacking, the herd closed in. The clang of cowbells marked their otherwise silent advance.

The pickup was only twenty feet away, but the herd stood between the men and the truck. Duke scooped up a large rock with a pointed end. He guessed it a fair implement for smashing in a cow's skull. His best choice at the moment.

The cows licked their lips and nostrils with purple, flaking tongues.

He raised the rock over his head and charged a white-and-brown Jersey. He swung the stone with all his weight and muscle behind it. It struck with a deafening crack, tearing away fur and skin, exposing the broken skull beneath. The cow lurched clumsily to one side. Grunting, Duke struck again. The cow bawled out a muted cry as her brainpan caved in. Duke glimpsed the brains beneath. Calling on what little supernatural strength he had, he unleashed a third blow. Bone shattered beneath stone, and the hit crushed the zombie's brains. The cow fell over in a twitching heap. She took his rock with her, firmly lodged in her skull.

But he didn't need it anymore. There was a hole in the herd's line. The truck (and its glove box) was an easy dash away.

Melinda charged from his right. Her fierce head butt to his hip knocked him flat on his ass. His vision blurred, he could barely see the hooves flailing at his face. He jerked clumsily out of the way, narrowly avoiding a braining.

Walter made a run for it. He zipped past two snapping zombies, but a third slammed him. He tumbled over the cow carcass. A Jersey bit a chunk out of his leg. His face twisted as he spit out a muffled groan.

Zombies nipped at Red's arms. They ripped his sleeves but didn't draw blood.

Melinda's slavering jaws dangled over Duke's face. He launched a punch at her nose. It landed in her mouth. She bit off his index and middle fingers. Blood dripped from her sagging lips as she casually chewed.

It hurt like hell, but the fingers would grow back. *If* he survived this ordeal. Werewolves could die by only specific circumstances: silver, fire, decapitation, some types of magic, and certain varieties of supernatural creatures. Getting eaten alive might make the list as well. He had never bothered to check.

Melinda swallowed with a satisfied slurp.

Betty leapt from the truck's bed. The dog fearlessly sprang upon the cow, sinking her teeth into Melinda's tender flank. A human zombie would've ignored the dog, but the freshly dead cows still retained a hint of bovine instinct. Melinda kicked Betty away. Betty spat out the shreds of skin and muscle. She bared her teeth, frothing at the mouth, and barking ferociously. The confused Jerseys backed away.

Duke and Red helped Walter to his feet. Duke practically hoisted Walt's wiry frame under one arm, and they ran to the truck. Walt and Red climbed into the cab. Duke hopped onto the bed. Walter jammed his key in the ignition. Red opened the glove box and found the revolver and a box of ammo. The bullets spilled onto the floor and across the seat. He grabbed up a handful and shoved them into the cylinder.

The cows' unnatural appetite overwhelmed their fear. Betty nipped at Melinda's ankles. A grazing kick glanced off her muzzle, sending her sprawling.

Walt started the truck and mashed the accelerator. The pickup peeled away, raising a cloud of dust.

Duke whistled. Betty jumped to her wobbly legs and dashed after the truck. Walt slowed down just enough to allow her to jump into the bed.

The zombies gave chase but quickly fell behind. Walter watched them become small dots in his rearview mirror before stopping.

"What the hell are you doing?" Red asked.

Walter took the thirty-eight and got out of the truck. He limped over to the tailgate and had a seat as the herd drew closer. He gave Duke his handkerchief.

"Sorry about your fingers there, son."

Duke wrapped his bloody hand. A red stain spread across the white cloth. "Ain't as bad as it looks."

Mooing, the ravenous zombies were almost within picking off range.

"They really were a good bunch of girls."

"I'd do it for you, but I'm left-handed."

Walt raised his revolver in two steady hands. "S'alright. I should do it. I owe 'em that much."

He squeezed off one well-aimed shot. The bullet punched a bloodless wound between a Jersey's eyes. It fell over. With single-minded determination, the rest of the herd trotted forward. Frowning, Walt put down the rest of the Jerseys. Five cows in five shots. The last zombie collapsed just six steps from her goal. Betty jumped from the bed and cautiously sniffed the corpses convulsing in the dirt.

"Is that normal?"

"Pretty much. How's your leg?"

Walter shrugged. "I've had worse. I ain't going to turn into a zombie, am I?"

"Doesn't work that way, usually, but if you wanna play it safe eat a lot of salt the next couple of days. That should clean out your system just fine."

"Don't you think we ought to get you fellas patched up?" Red shouted from the cab.

Walter dug a worn twenty dollar bill out of his wallet and threw in another twenty bucks for Duke's lost fingers. He climbed into the driver's seat.

"Betty, get your butt in gear!"

The dog snarled at one dead cow, barked at another, and ran back to the truck.

SEVEN

A werewolf's wounds healed according to when they were received. Once, Duke's chest had been blown open by a point-blank shotgun blast, but the damage had been done after dark during a full moon. He'd simply dusted himself off and gotten on with his evening. But his fingers had been bitten off around noon during the cycle of the new moon, and the digits were taking their sweet time in growing back.

He wiggled the knuckle-and-a-half that had regenerated so far. The loss forced him to eat his dinner with his off hand, which wasn't all that difficult, but still annoying, nonetheless.

Yawning, Earl emerged from the kitchen.

" 'Bout time you got yer ass up," Duke said between bites of chili.

The vampire fumbled around in his overalls' deep pockets and produced a comb. He took a seat on the stool beside Duke and ran the teeth through his thin hair. He combed it one way. Then another. Then another. Finally ending up with a laughable combover gracing his clearly bald head. Duke cut Earl a break. It may have been a ridiculous attempt, but at least Earl couldn't check himself in a mirror to realize how stupid it looked. Earl yawned again.

"You're teeth are out," Duke informed.

The vampire ran his tongue across his teeth and felt the bump of his extended fangs.

"Shit."

He turned away and grumbled at the undead bloodsucker's version of the embarrassing morning boner. Actually, vampires still got those as well, though not usually at the same time.

"C'mon. C'mon. That's it." Fangs retracted, he turned back. "Thanks. So you wanna tell me what happened to your fingers."

"Zombie cow."

"Longhorn?"

"Jersey."

Earl winced. "That's gotta be embarrassing. I mean, a big, badass werewolf like yourself gettin' his ass kicked by Bossie the milk cow."

"Funny."

"Or was it Bessie?"

Duke cracked his knuckles one at a time. Earl knew that to be a sign of dangerous annoyance but couldn't stop himself.

He snapped his fingers. "I got it. It had to be a Clarabell. Am I right?"

Duke's arm moved in a blur. Earl felt the sting of the spoon imbedded in his gut before he actually saw it.

"Damn it, Duke. This is my favorite shirt, you humorless prick."

He grabbed the two inches of handle sticking out and

tugged with little effect. He summoned a portion of his undead strength and pulled harder. The utensil held tight, and he
was reluctant to call upon more supernatural muscle for fear
of accidentally tearing a bigger hole in his shirt.

A few ounces of vampire blood, dull red and thick as mo-
lasses, oozed from the wound. Earl grabbed a napkin and wiped
it away.

His side began to tingle ever so slightly.

"Goddamn! That chili didn't have garlic in it, did it?"

"Just a touch," Duke replied.

The tingle grew into a light burning twinge.

Earl clutched his side and danced around in a panicky circle.
"Get it out! Get it out! Get it out!" The vampire hopped from
foot to foot. He grimaced.

Duke grabbed Earl by the shoulder and threw him against
the counter. "Quit your twitchin'."

"Be careful. It's my favorite shirt."

The werewolf extracted the spoon with a twist of his wrist.
A loud rip echoed through the diner as the overalls tore. Duke
tossed the utensil on the counter.

"I licked the spoon, you puss."

Earl put his finger through the tear in his clothes. "You
didn't have to do that. I loved this shirt. It makes my shoulders
look wider."

"Maybe next time you'll keep your mouth shut."

"You gotta admit. It's pretty funny."

"I could've been killed. Maybe."

"That's what makes it so funny."

Duke picked up the spoon and tapped it against the bowl.

"Alright already. Damn, you lose a couple of fingers and

your sense of humor with 'em. Not that you had much to be-gin with."

They took their seats back at the counter.

"Cows huh? How many?"

"Six."

Earl whistled. "That ain't good."

"And I don't think they were dead when they turned. They were too fresh. Whatever got into 'em, it got 'em when they were still alive."

"You don't think it's contagious, do you?"

"We burned the carcasses just to be safe, but Loretta has been burning her zombies. So that doesn't appear to be stopping it."

"Hell."

Both men knew what to expect if this continued to spread unchecked. Especially if it didn't limit itself to things already dead. Earl, being neither alive nor dead, and Duke, possessing unnatural powers of regeneration, were safely immune to zombiefication. The ordinary citizens of Rockwood were not.

"Maybe we should just move on," Earl suggested, "before things get . . . messy."

"Yep. Maybe we should."

Both knew they wouldn't. Whatever evil might be at work, only they stood a chance of stopping it. If they left now the good folks of Rockwood would surely be doomed. If not to transformation into a town of shambling zombies, then to am-munition shortages and plunging property values. Duke and Earl just couldn't do it.

Their gas tank was nearly empty, and they were flat broke.

"Guess it's time to call Hector."

Duke nodded. "Couldn't hurt."

Earl asked to use Loretta's phone. She quickly agreed when he explained it should help resolve the situation. The vampire took a seat by the phone with a notepad.

"Who's he calling?"

"Just this guy we know in El Paso," Duke replied. "He's a warlock."

"Metaphysical scholar," Earl corrected.

"Whatever. He knows all about this kind of stuff."

"That so? Then why didn't you call him before?"

"Didn't realize the seriousness of the situation."

"Don't worry about a thing. I'm sure once I explain things to Hec, he'll—Hey, Hec. It's Earl. We got a big walking corpse problem, and we were hoping maybe you could help us out."

While Earl carried out his thorough phone consultation, Loretta gave the floor a cursory mopping, and, having nothing better to do, Duke lent a hand. They worked in awkward silence broken only by the slap of brown mops against tile and Earl's half-conversation. Finally, much as Duke tried to avoid it, both wound up wringing out their mops at the same time.

Loretta wrung first. "I don't want you feeling uncomfortable about this morning. If anyone should be embarrassed about that, it's me." She chuckled. "I came on a little strong. Hell, I was worse than a two-dollar whore."

"Wasn't that bad," Duke replied.

"Yes, it was. The point is, I've got needs, but that don't give me any right to force them on you. I understand if a handsome young fella like yourself doesn't want to have anything to do with a woman of my . . . proportions."

An uncomfortable grunt rose from Duke's throat. "It ain't that."

"Now, now, I'm a grown woman. You don't gotta worry about hurting my feelings."

He dipped his mop in the bucket. She was right, of course. Somewhat. But there was more to it than that.

"Look. It ain't about that. You're a good woman, Loretta. And I'm, well, I am what I am."

She leaned closer and whispered. "You mean, you can't . . . perform?"

Duke recoiled. " 'Course I can perform. Pretty damn well, too. It's just my . . . uh . . . condition."

"Does that make it dangerous when you . . . ?"

"Yes. Yeah, see when I get too excited . . . things can get . . . risky."

It was an outright lie. He didn't transform against his will. His monstrous form was all rage and fury, designed to stalk and kill. It had nothing at all to do with carnal relations, but lying to her seemed the easiest way to get himself out of an uncomfortable situation.

"That's alright, Duke. I understand. It's no big thing." She scowled at the eternal red splotch. It always came off easy enough but never took five minutes to return.

"Thanks, Hector," Earl said. "I'll look into it and call you back." He hung up the phone.

"Well?" Loretta asked.

"He had some ideas, but I have to check some stuff out before we can be sure." He tucked the notebook under his arm and headed for the door. "I'll be back in a little while. And, oh yeah, Duke. Hec said getting eaten alive definitely would'a killed you."

"Thanks for askin'."

"No problem."

Earl considered grabbing a quick snack before going to the cemetery, but a vampire could go a while between meals. He wasn't hungry enough for cow's blood tonight.

Cathy the ghost was waiting in the graveyard as he knew she would be. The cemetery guardian had nowhere else to go and nothing else to do but wait. She was sitting on her plot, looking bored. A wide grin spread across her face when she noticed him. She jumped to her feet and waved vigorously.

"Hey! You came back!"

Earl nodded while flipping through his notes.

"I wasn't sure you would."

"Just checking things out."

She glanced over his shoulder. "Cool. What are you looking for? Maybe I can help."

"Thanks, but I can handle it."

Hector had suggested checking the easternmost tree first. The graveyard didn't have trees, only cacti, but Earl guessed that to be close enough. He knelt down and started digging.

"Is this still about the zombies?" Cathy asked.

"Yeah."

"What are you hoping to find?"

"Mojo bag."

"What's that?"

"It's kind'a hard to explain."

"Oh."

For a blessed few seconds, she stopped pestering him. Of course, her just being there was unsettling enough.

The ghost knelt beside him. "Can I ask you something?"

Earl sighed. "Yeah."

"What's it like being a vampire?"

He shrugged. "It's really not much different than being human."

"Oh."

She sounded disappointed. The reaction was typical. Most people expected more, but the truth was, with the exception of a few lifestyle changes, his existence hadn't changed much since joining the ranks of the undead.

"Are you really immortal?"

"I don't age."

"And what about mirrors? That's not true, is it?"

"It's true."

"Wow. So you can't see your reflection?"

"I can see my clothes. I just can't see me. It's sort of like the invisible man, 'cept only in mirrors."

She grinned. "Cool. Um, can I ask you something else?"

He stopped digging. "Yes, garlic bothers me. Yes, sunlight can kill me. No, crosses and holy water don't do jack shit. At least not to me. Yes, I can cross running water. No, a stake in the heart doesn't kill me, but it does keep me from moving around. Yes, having my head cut off or being roasted can kill me. Yes, I sleep during the day. Yes, I drink blood. No, I can enter without being invited. And yes, I can mesmerize people, though not very well. Does that cover it?"

"Uh . . . yeah, I guess. I'm sorry. Am I bothering you?"

She certainly was, but much as he wanted to tell her to go away, he couldn't bring himself to. He had no idea how long she'd been here, how many years she'd been condemned to watch over this forsaken lot of dirt with only the dead to keep her company. And now, not even that. One way or another, he'd be leaving Rockwood soon, and Cathy would be alone again for a long stretch of eternity.

"Sorry. I'm just in a bad mood 'cuz I got stabbed earlier." The wound had already closed, but a twinge rippled through his side still, thanks to the traces of garlic on the spoon. "Go ahead. Ask me anything you want."

"So crosses don't really affect you?"

"Not me personally. I've met some others that were bothered by 'em, but I'm an atheist." He checked his hole in the dirt. "Guess it's not here."

"Why do you think it would be there?"

"It's gotta be the easternmost cactus."

"This isn't the easternmost cactus. It's that one over there."

Earl squinted where she pointed. He could've sworn this was east, but then again, his sense of direction had always been unreliable at best.

"Thanks."

Buried about a foot deep beside the real easternmost cactus, he found what he was looking for. It was a cheap purse filled with strange and exotic items. The bag was a black-magic fetish, the channel through which dark powers entered the cemetery. Now that it was dug up, there would be no more zombies coming from this particular graveyard.

"Oh that," Cathy said.

"You knew about this?"

"Sure. I saw the guy who buried it."

"What'd he look like?"

"I don't remember exactly. I was sitting by my grave at the time, and I didn't bother getting up to get a closer look. I think he was a kid. Maybe sixteen, seventeen years old."

"How long ago did he bury it?"

"A while. I don't know exactly. I've sort of lost my sense of time."

It was understandable. Ghosts were timeless beings.

"See you later."

"You're going. Already?"

"I found what I was looking for." He rattled the purse.

"Can't you stay just a little while longer?"

"I really shouldn't. I got stuff to do."

"Oh. Okay. Well, can I ask one last favor before you go? Can I touch you? I haven't touched anyone in years. Just a handshake."

He held out his hand.

Carefully, almost reverently, she put her hand in his and squeezed softly. Her ectoplasmic flesh felt cool to the touch. Earl didn't find it as repulsive as he normally did. He allowed the contact to linger for a few moments longer than he would have liked before finally slipping free.

"You know, it's been so long since I've done that, I'd forgotten what it felt like."

"Well, like I said, I got stuff to do."

"Will I see you again?"

"Yeah. How 'bout tomorrow night?" His reply surprised him.

Eyes wide, she beamed. "Really?"

He grinned back. "Yeah. Sure."

"That's great!" She leapt on him, wrapping her arms tightly around him.

Earl didn't push her away. Nor did the urge even strike him.

She let go. Her cheeks paled in a ghostly blush. "So I'll see you tomorrow then."

He couldn't look her in the eye. He glanced at his shuffling feet instead.

"Yeah. Tomorrow."

Earl didn't know why he'd made the promise. Even more unexplainable, he didn't know why he planned on keeping it.

EIGHT

The horn blared.

Grabbing her backpack, Tammy jumped off the couch and headed toward the door. "That's my ride."

"Just a moment there, young lady," her father croaked. "It's eight o'clock. Just where do you think you're going at this hour?"

"Chad and I are going to study together."

Her mother spoke without looking up from her knitting. "Have fun, dear."

"Now hold on a minute. Why can't you study here? Is there something wrong with this house? Are you ashamed of your parents?"

"No, Dad."

"Mind your tone, girl."

"Sorry, Dad."

A fumble momentarily distracted him. He shouted at the television.

"Oh, Sam, let the girl go."

He leaned back in his worn, creaky recliner. "Have you got your math book?"

"Yes," Tammy sighed.

He snorted.

She pulled the book from the backpack for him to see.

The horn honked again.

"Be back by eleven-thirty."

"Yes, Dad."

"Tammy, I mean it."

An icy chill crept into her voice. "Yes, sir."

"Have fun, dear," her mother said between the incessant clicking of needles.

On her way out, Tammy made sure to slam the door because she knew how much it irritated her father. She didn't care for Sam much. He wasn't that big of a jerk. Better than a lot of her friends' dads. But she was Mistress Lilith, Queen of Night, and it was hard enough to resurrect the old gods without having to deal with curfews, groundings, and math homework. She didn't know what the big deal was. A C-plus was passing. Maybe she wasn't "living up to her potential," as he so often put it, in geometry, but in the new age geometry would mean little. Denise Calhoun had a straight-A average. It wouldn't save her from the special hell Tammy had in store for pig-faced sluts who thought they were so smart just because they knew all about planes and points and parallel lines and other completely stupid stuff that nobody ever used in real life.

Tammy stopped at the curb and scowled at the yellow Gremlin waiting to whisk her away. She threw open the door.

"Goddamn it, you stupid son of a bitch."

Chad smiled stupidly. "What's wrong, babe?"

"I thought you were going to borrow your parents' truck?"

"Oh, well, I couldn't swing that. But I gave my brother ten bucks, and he let me borrow his car." His smile widened, transforming from stupid to downright idiotic. He revved the engine. It banged and popped and belched a large cloud that smelled of burning oil. "It's a hatchback."

She flopped into the passenger seat and slammed the door. Chad struggled with the gearshift for a while, eventually grinding his way to first.

Tammy slouched in her seat, propped her feet on the dashboard, and pulled out her geometry book and penlight. She studied on the way. There was much to do tonight and getting it all done before eleven-thirty was going to be difficult.

Chad put his hand on her knee. "So what's the plan tonight, baby?"

She smacked his fingers with her penlight. "Quit it. I'm trying to study here."

"Damn it. I was just asking."

"Just drive."

He grumbled under his breath. "You can be such a bitch, sometimes."

"What?"

"Nuthin'," he quietly replied, sucking his stinging knuckles. "Nuthin', Mistress Lilith."

Tammy said nothing, but Chad wouldn't be scoring tonight. She knew it. He knew it.

He switched on the radio. "Oh, hell."

Forty-five minutes later, the Gremlin pulled up to the gates of McAllister Fields, the largest defunct cemetery in the county. Chad killed the engine but left on the headlights. He and Tammy went to the gates, locked by a heavy padlock and a thick chain.

"Did you bring the bolt cutters like I told you?" she asked.

"Uh . . . no, but I've got this." He held up a crowbar.

"Jesus, you can be such a dumbass."

"No. It'll work. Look." He adopted a batting stance. "You better stand back, babe."

He struck a powerful smack against the lock. Metal clanged against metal. The padlock swayed on its chain with only a tiny scratch to mark the assault.

Tammy pulled her abridged *Necronomicon* from her backpack and, with great irritation, flipped through the pages.

Chad unleashed a relentless barrage on the stubborn padlock. Blow after blow rained, but, dented and scraped, the lock held. He wheezed, wiping the sweat away from his face.

"I think . . . I almost . . . it's ready to . . . any second now . . . babe."

She pushed him aside. Arms outstretched toward the gate, she chanted the Invocation of the Opened Way. It took five minutes to complete. On the utterance of the last syllable, the lock clicked open.

"I must've loosened it. So what are we here for, babe?"

"Bodies."

He paled. "But . . . but . . . I didn't think we needed bodies to make zombies."

"We don't. We're not making zombies anymore. We only need a couple," she reassured. "Four or five."

Chad froze. His upper lip twitched.

"C'mon, dumbass. We don't got all night."

He shook his head very slowly. "No way. No way. I'm not touching any dead guys."

"Yes, you are." She put her hands on her hips and tapped her foot impatiently.

"No, I'm not, and you can't make me."

"Don't be such a wuss."

"No way."

Tammy was prepared for such a reaction. He'd nearly wet his pants the time they'd had to collect the finger bones of a hanged man. His adolescent fear of the dead was yet another obstacle between her and destiny.

"Fine."

She set down her backpack and removed a Coke bottle. She twisted off the cap and ran her fingers up and down the length of the neck.

"If you don't want to, you don't have to."

She brought the bottle almost to her mouth and moistened her lips with her tongue.

Chad's horny teenage knees wobbled.

Tammy wrapped her lips around the bottle and took a long, long drink. A drop dribbled down her chin. She pulled away the bottle slowly and wiped away the drop with a deeply satisfied smile.

"Okay. Four dead guys, but I'm not touching any more."

She moistened her fingertip with the droplets on the bottle's rim and sucked it dry. "Five."

"Okay, but only five."

Tammy smiled. Boys were so easy.

She'd picked McAllister Fields for a very simple reason. It

was the closest cemetery that had aboveground crypts. It was so much easier to collect bodies when you didn't have to dig them up. She lucked out even more as the first crypt wasn't even locked. Chad used his crowbar to pry open the coffin inside. He recoiled from the stench of fetid flesh and retreated to a corner to vomit.

Tammy glanced over the corpse. "She'll do."

Chad wiped his lips and leaned over the open coffin. "What do we need them for, anyway?"

"Quit asking stupid questions and take her to the car."

Squeamish delicacy pummeled beneath the raging fists of surging hormones, he lifted the corpse over his shoulder. He gagged, inhaling a thick dust cloud that smelled like moldy cotton and reminded him of grandma. The body's pinkie finger snapped off with a dry crack.

"Be careful, moron," Tammy snarled.

Their task went smoothly. Chad's repulsion faded to mere discomfort by the time the fifth body was loaded in the back of the Gremlin. It was a tight fit. Huffing and cursing, he wedged the cargo in and slammed the hatchback shut, accidentally chopping off a dangling leg just below the knee.

"Shit."

"Come on already," Tammy growled from the passenger's seat. She glared with the aid of the rearview mirror.

He bent down so that she couldn't see him and considered the limb laying in the dirt.

"Is there a problem?"

"No. No, it's cool."

He tossed the leg into the night's darkness. If she asked him about it, he'd just say the corpse had already been missing it. It was a poor ruse and doomed to failure. But his lust gave him the barest of hopes that she might believe him. He wasn't scoring tonight, but a half-hour grope session was still a heartening possibility.

The grind of wheels in the dusty road announced the approach of a brown police car. Chad froze before its headlights. Sheriff Kopp stepped from the vehicle. He shone a flashlight into Chad's stymied eyes.

"Chad Roberts, is that you?"

Stiffly, Chad nodded. This was it. They were finally busted. He'd always known it would happen eventually. You couldn't run around graveyards and summon the powers of darkness, even in a place like Rockwood, for long without drawing attention. The cult was over. His dad would whup his ass. His mom would frown in that quietly disapproving way of hers. He'd probably get expelled and might even go to jail for desecrating the dead. He wasn't sure that was a crime, but it seemed like it should be.

Well, he mused, at least I got some action out of it. And while Tammy could be a real Grade A superbitch more often than not, she was one fine piece of ass. He had no regrets.

Sheriff Kopp strode over and opened the Gremlin's door. "Alright now, young lady, step out of the car."

Tammy did as she was asked. The tall, lean man towered over the short seventeen-year-old.

"You wanna tell me what you kids are doing out here?"

She craned her neck all the way back to look him in the face, squinting in the point-blank glare of his flashlight.

"Nuthin', sir."

"Nuthin', sir," Chad echoed. His voice cracked.

Sheriff Kopp moved toward Chad, who quickly stepped forward and away from the Gremlin. Kopp was not fooled.

"Stay put, boy."

"Yes, sir."

Chad's heart thumped noisily. His stomach churned. His bladder suddenly felt excruciatingly full.

Behind Kopp, Tammy, eyes closed, was mumbling inaudibly.

The sheriff scanned the Gremlin's interior with a sweep of his flashlight. He frowned ever so slightly at the five bodies piled in the back.

"Looks to me like you kids got some explainin' to do."

The statement was powerful in its understatement. Too powerful for Chad to stand against.

"She made me do it! I didn't want to do it! I didn't!" Tears welled up in his eyes. "She's a witch! She's got these weird powers. She hypnotized me! Yeah, that's what she did!"

Sheriff Kopp looked Tammy's svelte form up and down. "I just bet she did. Okay, into the back of the squad car. I don't want any trouble from you two." He gently, yet firmly, guided them toward his automobile.

Tammy spun around and held her hands in Kopp's face. She had to stand on her tiptoes.

"Shurma'laka'rala'kama, Lord of Dreams, Master of Souls, I invoke thee."

Sheriff Kopp shuddered and stopped.

"There's nothing going on here," Tammy said, "Everything's fine. Nothing needs explaining. In fact, none of this ever happened. Now get in your car and go away."

Sheriff Kopp's expression became normal, save for a certain vague dullness behind his eyes. He climbed into his cruiser.

"You kids better get yourself home. It's getting late." He started the car and drove off without another word.

"Wow! That was awesome. I didn't know you could do that!"

Tammy socked Chad directly in the solar plexus.

"You asshole."

"What is that?" he asked between coughs. "Some kind of mind control thing. Like in *Star Wars*, right?"

She sneered. "Let's get out of here."

"You aren't mad about that whole 'she made me do it' act, are you, babe?" he asked as they drove back. "I was just distracting him for you. So you could do your Jedi mind trick on him." He grinned. "Man, that was so fucking cool!"

She stared at her geometry book with burning intensity.

"Can you show me how to do that?"

No reply was given. Ten minutes passed.

"How come you don't just use that hocus-pocus on Loretta so we can get into the diner?"

"It doesn't work on everyone, and only for a short while when it does," she answered through clenched teeth.

Chad nodded to himself for the next couple of minutes.

"Aw c'mon, Mistress Lilith. I was just trying to distract him. Really."

She slammed her book shut with a sharp slap.

Chad admitted defeat. No groping tonight. Especially after she found out about the missing leg.

Oh well, he thought as he drew once more from the bottomless well of throbbing teenage desire, maybe tomorrow.

NINE

Earl spilled the mojo bag's contents across the counter. He sorted through the odd collection of items, both mundane and exotic.

Loretta picked up an empty pepper shaker. "This is mine."

"It's gotta be the connection to the diner. So the zombies know to attack this place."

"What about the rest of this stuff?"

"Mostly magical ingredients. A cock's left claw. A black tail feather from the same chicken. Some mushrooms plucked from a corpse."

"And this?" She held up a scrap of paper with some indecipherable writing.

"That's an invocation," Duke replied. "Looks like Glok'rooshah, Prince of Shadows. Or maybe Fuyirbahga, He That Corrupts The Flesh."

Earl and Loretta tossed him suspicious looks.

"Last time we were in El Paso, I looked through Hector's

library." He took the paper and read the scribbles. "Rise, Fuyirbahga. From the bowels of the earth, I bid thee, seep into this place of death and bring forth the rotted flesh to purge the unbelievers."

Earl snatched back the paper. "You're making that up."

"That's what it says."

"Bullshit."

"Read it yourself."

The vampire squinted at the writing. "Eyes-ray. Rum-fray ee-thay owls-bay of-ay ee-thay urth-ay." He snarled. "What is it? Greek? Sanskrit?"

"Pig Latin," Loretta replied.

"Yup," Duke confirmed. "Secret language of the old gods."

Earl chuckled. "That's stupid."

"No. It's smart. Think about it. Everybody knows it. Nobody thinks nuthin' 'bout it. But it's out there, everywhere, just waiting for somebody who knows how to use it."

"It's still stupid."

"Maybe. But it works."

"So that's it?" Loretta asked. "Now that this is dug up, there won't be any more zombies?"

"That's what Hec said."

"What about the cows?"

"Hec figured they got infected with some black-magic runoff by accident. Happens sometimes with especially powerful hoodoo."

Loretta breathed a sigh of relief. "That's great. I wanna thank you boys for your—"

"Hold up a minute. This might not be over yet."

"But I thought this got rid of the zombies."

"It did, but whoever planted this in the cemetery is still out there. And for whatever reason, they got it out for your place. Or something in this place. Maybe even you. Now that the zombies are gone, they might—just might, mind you—try something else."

"Hell," Loretta grumbled.

"You got any idea who might be interested in driving you outta business?"

"Nobody that I know of."

"That's gonna make things harder. Until we find whoever is responsible for this, it could keep happening."

Loretta took a moment to wrestle with her tangled yellow hair. "Somebody in this town is practicing voodoo?"

"Voodoo is a religion," Duke interrupted.

She pinned back the stringy, bleached mass. "Yeah?"

"So voodoo is a real religion. People who practice it don't do stuff like that any more than Baptists or Catholics do."

"Exactly," Earl agreed. "We're not talking about Voodoo or Wicca or even Satanism. All those are pretty much harmless. No, what we got here is a genuine black-magic practitioner, a true disciple of the old gods. And a damn powerful one at that."

"Old gods?" Loretta asked.

"Long story. Let's just say that they make Beelzebub look like a bald, toothless rat with one leg and leave it at that."

"Think there might be more than one?" Duke said.

"Usually are."

"Hold on a second here. So there's a person or persons calling up the powers of Hell just to run me outta business?"

They nodded.

"We're talking about a cult or sumthin'?"

They nodded again.

"In Rockwood? But we don't even got a movie theater."

"That's how it usually works. People who got stuff to do don't usually sign up with the minions of darkness. It's the folks with lots'a time to kill that you gotta watch out for."

"Idle hands," Duke agreed.

"So you've seen this kind of thing before?"

"All the time," Earl replied, "especially in isolated, quiet little places like this." He leaned closer. "If you're ever in New Mexico, don't pick up any hitchhikers. Better than fifty-fifty chance you'll wind up strapped to an altar."

"You're making that up."

"Happened to me twice. Swear to God."

She snorted skeptically and returned to the original subject. "You figure Gil's disappearance is related to all this?"

"I got that feeling."

"But he was such a harmless ol' guy. Why'd somebody want to hurt him?"

"Why would someone want to hurt you?" posed Earl. "People do nasty things to each other. Don't usually have a good reason for it."

She nodded. "Okay. How are we supposed to find this cult?"

"You know this town better than us. You got any candidates?"

She paced behind the counter, rubbing her flapping chin thoughtfully. "Well, there's old Curtis Mayfair. He's always been an odd fella. Lives by himself in an old shack. Don't come into town much. Always talking to his dog about astrophysics or sumthin'."

"Wouldn't be him," Earl said. "See, these cults are clever. They don't act weird like that. They blend in, act just like regular folks except for the occasional orgy or human sacrifice. Odds are, you probably talked to whoever is doing this and didn't even know it."

"So it could be anybody except for ol' Curtis."

"We can't just eliminate him either. See, sometimes an especially clever practitioner acts crazy on purpose because they know no one thinks the weirdo is really a cultist. They're tricky that way.

"Practitioners are hard to pick out because they're not like Duke or me. There's signs of our conditions if you know what to look for, but we're talking about normal people here. Completely regular humans who consort with darkness. It's hard to pin them down unless you're lucky enough to catch them in the act. We just gotta keep our eyes open. Now that we know what we're looking for, it's just a matter of time."

Scowling, Loretta drummed her fingers on the counter.

"On the bright side," Earl comforted, "maybe the zombies are all they got."

"You think?"

"Probably not," he answered honestly.

She slapped a fist into a palm with a meaty smack.

"Damnation . . ."

TEN

First thing in the morning, Loretta called Gonzalez General Repair. Wanda Gonzalez, a middle-aged Mexican with skin like leather, arrived a little before noon and quietly went to replacing the shattered glass doors.

Sometime soon after, Sheriff Kopp popped in for a visit. He nodded to Wanda. Wanda, a pane of glass under arm, nodded back.

"Sheriff," Duke greeted.

"Morning, Mr. Smith," Kopp returned, removing his dusty hat. "Loretta around?"

"She's in back."

Kopp took a seat at the counter, a few stools down from Duke. The sheriff studied the brim of his Stetson for a few minutes while whistling some lazy tune Duke didn't recognize.

"Heard you had a little trouble yesterday."

"Nuthin' I couldn't handle."

"Ol' Walt Hastings said you lost a couple of fingers."

"Naw." Duke held up his left hand and wiggled his freshly grown digits. "It looked worse than it was."

"I'm sure Walter will be glad to hear that."

A long quiet fell upon the diner, broken only by the clink of Wanda's work.

"Walt said you smashed open a cow's skull with a rock. I gotta say that's impressive. Damn impressive."

"It was a big rock."

"Just the same, I don't know of many men who could manage that. You ever work with livestock, Mr. Smith?"

"Nope."

"My daddy had a couple. When I was a kid, I use'ta milk 'em. I had this special rod: a big, heavy lead one. The kind of rod that'd crack open a man's skull just like that." He snapped his fingers. "We used it to keep the cows in line. I'd whomp on 'em when they got ornery. Hit 'em as hard as I could. Just to keep 'em in line. Never did much to the cows except annoy 'em."

"That right?"

"Yeah. So I figure a man would have to be God-awful strong to smash open a cow's thick head. Even with a big rock."

"Took three blows."

"Just the same, mighty impressive."

Duke took a long sip of his Coke.

The sheriff whistled a second verse.

Duke had encountered the likes of Marshall Kopp before: the quiet, thoughtful sort of man who knew more than he'd ever come right out and say. Duke decided to stop screwing around.

"I'm a werewolf."

Kopp went to the cooler and grabbed a soda. "Figured it was sumthin' like that."

"How'd you know?"

"Oh, I've had plenty of experience with this sort of thing. 'Bout seven years back, had an outbreak of vampire turkeys. And four years before that, Charlie Vaughn's daughter got herself possessed. And the Stillmans's scarecrow took to wandering around at night and scaring the bejeezus outta the kids. Point is, Rockwood has itself an unusual history, and being sheriff means dealing with those problems." Kopp cocked his head to glance at Duke with a carefully calculated half-stare meant to appear casual, but was anything but. "You ain't going to be a problem, are you, Mr. Smith?"

"No, sir."

"Glad to hear it. And you can call me 'Marshall.' Everybody does."

Loretta's wide, jiggling frame emerged from the back. They exchanged polite nods.

"What can I do for you, Marshall?"

"Sorry to have to do this to you, Loretta, but I gotta ask you to close this place up."

"What for?"

"C'mon now," the sheriff sighed. "Y'know it's my job to look after the people of this county. I was willing to overlook the zombies as long as they kept to bothering you, but now with Walt's cows getting infected . . ."

"That ain't my fault."

"Yeah. But this whole walking corpse trouble started with this diner, and I have'ta figure it's connected some way."

"That's not fair, Marshall, and you know it."

"Fair or not, I can't have the dead shambling around and pestering my citizens."

"But I took care of the zombies." Loretta reached under the counter and placed the dusty mojo bag before the sheriff. "This here is what was making 'em."

Kopp flipped through the purse. "Ah hell. Not another cult."

"'Fraid so," Duke confirmed.

"Another cult?" Loretta asked.

"Yeah. Seems like one pops up every couple of years. It's gotta be the heat."

"You need a movie theater," Duke observed.

"I've been trying to get a public swimmin' pool."

"That'd help."

Wanda finished with the doors, and Loretta paid her bill in cash.

"You want me to order up another set?" Wanda asked.

"Thanks, but I won't be needing 'em."

The handywoman puffed on her cigarette stub. "Think I'll order 'em anyway. Just in case."

She packed up her tools. Loretta returned to the original topic of conversation. "Anyway, according to the boys, now that this is dug up, everything will finally quiet down."

"Guess I can give you another chance," Sheriff Kopp said, "but this is it. If anything funny happens, I'm gonna have to shut you down. Nuthin' personal, Loretta."

"I know, Marshall. Just doin' your job." She held up a large rectangle of cardboard with big black letters across it.

NOW 100% ZOMBIE FREE. ASK ABOUT THE BOTTOMLESS CUP OF COFFEE: ONLY 25¢.

"What do you think?"

"Nice," Kopp replied.

"It'll do until I scrape up enough to rent the billboard by the interstate."

The sheriff tucked the bag under his arm. "I'll take this for evidence if that's alright with you." He tipped his hat. "I gotta be going. Somebody stole some bodies from McAllister Fields. Probably related to all this. Least, I hope it's related. Hate to think we got both grave robbers and a cult running around."

He dropped seventy-five cents for the soda.

"I haven't met your friend yet, Mr. Smith."

"He sleeps during the day."

The sheriff smiled crookedly. "Then I'll just have to drop by tonight. See you around, Loretta, Mr. Smith."

Kopp moseyed out of the diner with a generous swagger.

The nearest restaurant-supply store was a good four-hour drive there and back. Loretta persuaded Duke to come along and keep her company. He agreed reluctantly, worried about the awkward quiet that might fill the cab. His concerns were quickly put aside. Whether she bought his werewolf excuse or not, Loretta seemed to be handling the rejection well.

The truck skimmed down the interstate. Brief moments of conversation were broken by long moments of silence. Not the cumbersome, unpleasant sort of silence, but the absolute calm of two people who didn't feel the need to fill every second with noise. Occasionally, Loretta would throw out some polite comment about the weather, and Duke would nod or shake his head as the situation required.

After exhausting every possible variation of "Hot 'nuff for ya?" Loretta couldn't resist indulging her curiosity.

"Mind if I ask you a personal question? It's about your condition."

"Nope."

"How'd you get it?"

He tugged the brim of his baseball cap lower over his eyes. "I killed a werewolf. That's how you become one. 'He who slays the beast inherits its heart.' Least, that's the prettiest way I've heard it put."

"You killed a werewolf?"

"I ran him over with an eighteen-wheeler. It was dark, and I wasn't paying enough attention to the road, and he just darted out in front of me and those rigs don't stop on a dime. Ended up mashing the poor bastard's head flat as a wafer. Ain't exactly decapitation, but I guess it was close enough. Anyway, I climbed outta the truck. By then, he'd gone back to being a naked human."

"What did you do?"

"I got back in my truck and got the hell out of there."

"You didn't wait for help?"

"Aren't any doctors that I know of able to fix a mashed skull, and I'd just gotten my CDL. Didn't want to screw up my life 'cuz I flattened a naked guy running through the woods in the middle of the night."

Loretta frowned. "Doesn't seem right."

"It wasn't right, but it was what I did. Still don't know his name or even what he looked like, but he was a werewolf alright."

"So you just knew that you'd become one?"

"Not 'til the next full moon. Now that stuff about the moon affecting werewolves is only half true. I get stronger with the full moon, but I don't have to change if I don't want. But I was just a kid, and I didn't even know I'd become what I was. I get in this bar fight over a turn at the pool table. This biker breaks a cue over my head, and I lose control. I change right there in front of everyone. Scared the living shit outta everybody, including me." He chuckled. "Good thing, too. I was so freaked out that I ran off instead of killing everyone in the place.

"Spent a couple of months on the move after that, changin' every full moon, thinking I couldn't get close to anyone 'cuz I might end up ripping out their hearts. Werewolves can't hold that stuff in. It just kept building and building until I finally found this guy alone in the woods and tore into him."

Quietly disapproving, she shook her head.

"So I've ripped him to shreds, and I'm hunched over his gutted corpse, gnawing on his intestines. Which tasted like shit. So I snap off a hunk of innards and choke it down 'cuz I figure that's what I'm s'posed to do. And I get this picture of how my life is gonna be. Eating rotten intestines, stalking through the woods, barfing up rotten intestines, throwing myself under an eighteen-wheeler on a lonely stretch of interstate."

"You seem alright now," Loretta observed.

"I was just gettin' to that. I stop chewing on the guy long enough to gag, and when I turn back, he's busy shoving his guts back in. He gives me the hairy eyeball, and asks me to help him find his pancreas."

Duke smiled widely or as wide as he ever did, which was wide enough for someone to notice without making a big deal of it.

"It was Earl."

"That when you first met?"

"Yeah. He helped me unlearn every wrong thing horror movies had ever taught me. Probably saved my life."

Quiet fell upon the pickup and lasted for a little over nineteen minutes.

"Is that why you hang around with him?" Loretta asked. " 'Cuz he saved your life?"

"Sort'a. I know Earl isn't always easy to get along with. Fact is, he can be a real pain in the ass more often than not, but after you spend enough time with him, and you learn to ignore his personality, he's a pretty decent guy."

"If you say so."

"Plus it ain't easy being a monster in this world. Helps to have someone around who understands, somebody who can give you a hand when things get complicated."

"That happen a lot?"

"More often than it should. When you cross over into the weird stuff, there's no going back. Hector has a theory on it. Calls it the law of 'Anomalous Phenomena Attraction.' He explained it to me once. Didn't really pay close attention, but it boils down to 'weird shit pulls in more weird shit.' Figure it's gotta be true. Ever since I killed that guy, I keep runnin' across cults and monsters and fallen gods."

"So this sort'a thing happens a lot."

He snorted deeply and spat a wad of phlegm out the window.

"All the damn time."

And another long silence descended on the pickup.

ELEVEN

Tammy whiled away every study hall engaged in the complex and often seemingly impenetrable science of the arcane. Even for one of her considerable occult talent, it was a difficult task. It was a chore she did not particularly care for, but the rewards it would eventually bring kept her at it. The key to unlocking the old gods required that just the right ritual be performed at just the right time in just the right place by just the right person. It wasn't easy deciphering important heavenly movements when the best reference book available was her mother's three-volume astrology collection. And the records of ancient Atlantis were absurd in their verbosity. And Mrs. Richards didn't make things any easier.

The wrinkled, old teacher cleared her throat.

"May I ask what your doing?"

Tammy closed her notebook. "Nuthin'."

"May I see that please?"

Sighing, Tammy handed over her sacred notebook. Mrs.

Richards glanced through the pages. She had no idea of the importance of what she looked at. To such an unenlightened fool, the secrets of the universe were little more than the scrawlings of a stupid, teenage girl. It helped that Tammy made it a practice to dot all her "i"s and "j"s with little hearts and smiley faces. The hearts were those ripped from the breasts of all foolish enough to stand in her way. The smiley faces just made the notes prettier.

"What did I tell you about this?"

"I'm sorry, ma'am."

"I told you I'd take this away if I saw it again."

"I'm sorry. I'll put it away."

"This is the last time." The old hag looked down her nose at Tammy. "This is study hall. I want to see some studying. Am I making myself clear, young lady?"

Tammy struggled not to scowl and managed a not-quite-hidden frown. "Yes, Mrs. Richards."

"Very good."

Mrs. Richards returned to her desk in the front of the room.

"Uck-fay oo-yay, oo-yay old-ay at-bay," Tammy grumbled.

The slate blackboard shuddered, and a single long crack split down its middle.

The class filled with murmuring students. Mrs. Richards shushed everyone with a hard glare and explained away the incident as the foundation settling.

Chad, who sat three rows away from Tammy, passed a note through a chain of students.

"Are we doing anything tonight?" it inquired.

She sent back her reply. "Yes. And bring your mom's good silverware."

He read it and grimaced.

Tammy reached under her desk and pulled out her English book. She pretended to read it while she mused on the approaching fate of the world in general, and Mrs. Richards in particular.

TWELVE

Rockwood didn't have a movie theater or an IHOP or a strip mall. But it did have two churches, a ramshackle bar, and last (but certainly not least) Wacky Willie's Deluxe Goofy Golf, a barren landscape of wilted ferns and plastic flamingos with peeling paint. Wacky Willie had added the "Deluxe" when finally ridding the thirteenth hole windmill of a stubborn family of bats after a great and terrible struggle that would forever be known as "The Fearsome Bat War of Rockwood County" to Willie, but was usually referred to as "That Time Willie Had To Get Rabies Shots" by everyone else. At night, the lights would go on and every june bug and mosquito (and once a swarm of locusts) in a hundred miles would flock to worship before their halogen altar with the inevitable unfortunate hair tangling incident. Insect graveyards littered the ground around the lights. Wacky Willie's Deluxe Goofy Golf was broken down and overpriced, but as it was the only activity available within fifty miles (other than church socials, heavy drinking, and junkyard rat shoots) it had become a thriving recreational hub of Rockwood. And any sort of hub in Rockwood was bound to have a rich and unusual history.

There was the ghost of Herbert Smythe. A lifetime devotee of Wacky Willie's Goofy Golf, Herbert's heart had given out on the eighteenth hole as he prepared to shoot the final hole-in-one of a perfect game. Popular legend went that on quiet nights when the desert was still and no one was watching, Herbert would appear and play a round or two.

There was also the time that Joey Hill lost his ball in the mouth of the plywood alligator of hole sixteen and nearly got his arm bitten off as the reptile seemingly came to life for one impossible minute. Hole sixteen still swallowed a couple of balls a night, and these snacks, never to be seen again, were always its to keep.

There was that month when the purple people eater of hole four had spontaneously combusted and burned for one solid month before extinguishing just as spontaneously. The fire left the eater relatively unharmed, save for the word "Repent" scorched over its three eyes.

These incidents were a mere sampling of the many inexplicable events at Wacky Willie's. Willie had pamphlets made for the tourists. He'd even sold one which, at an asking price of five bucks, was something of an inexplicable event in itself.

Given its history, it was to be expected that Earl and Duke might be drawn to Wacky Willie's. This had little, if anything at all, to do with the law of Anomalous Phenomena Attraction and everything to do with the law of crushing boredom.

The pickup pulled into the gravel parking lot.

"This is stupid," Earl grunted.

Duke got out and walked toward the slanted wooden hut where customers rented their balls and clubs.

Earl stuck his head out the window and shouted. "Why can't we just go get a beer?"

The werewolf kept walking.

"Christ Almighty." Grumbling, the vampire climbed out of the truck and ran after him. "They got a bar, Duke."

"I'm trying not to drink, Earl."

"Oh, c'mon, one beer ain't gonna do nuthin'. And even if it does, so you sleep with Loretta. You could probably use a good lay anyway."

They stepped up to the admission shack. Wacky Willie himself sat in the thin, unvarnished box. His hair and beard were long and stringy. A thick mustache hid his mouth. His skin, what little of it that was visible under his woolly face, was pockmarked and flaking. His mustache writhed about in a decidedly non-wacky way as he smacked his lips at his two new customers.

"Two please," Duke requested.

"Twelve bucks."

"Twelve bucks?" Earl grumbled.

Willie nodded. His eyes bounced up and down a few moments longer than his head. "Got a discount plan. Fifty bucks for ten games in advance."

"We just need two."

Methodically, Willie set two clubs, two colored golf balls, and a scorecard before them.

"Got a pencil?" Earl asked.

Willie shrugged.

"How are we supposed to keep score?"

Willie offered another, less enthusiastic shrug.

Earl muttered something along the lines of "overpriced shit-hole."

"You boys care for a pamphlet? Only five dollars." Somewhere, deep in Willie's eyes, a spark of life shone.

"I'll give you a quarter," Duke bartered.

"Two dollars," Willie returned.

"Fifty cents."

"Deal." He handed over a pamphlet and pocketed his change.

Duke passed the pamphlet to Earl as they proceeded to the first hole. It was a busy night. Three families were already on the course. The werewolf set his yellow ball on the tee while Earl had a seat on a wobbly, splinter-ridden bench and leafed through the brochure.

"Says here nineteen people have been struck by lightning while playing hole seven."

"That a fact?"

Duke tapped his ball. It bounced across the torn, uneven felt, between the mummy's legs, and round a sharp corner to fall in the cup.

"Lucky shot," Earl remarked as he set his own tee.

He slapped the ball with his putter. The green sphere shot in the air, ricocheted off the mummy's knee, and landed in a potted fern.

Duke chuckled.

"That doesn't count. I was just warming up."

Earl set the ball back down and gave it a light tap. It rolled a few inches down the green before swinging back and settling to rest by Earl's feet.

"Do over."

"Excuse me."

The ghost of Herbert Smythe, who Earl had been stubbornly pretending not to see, stepped forward.

"If you want to make this hole, give the ball a light tap and bounce it right here. Even if you don't make it, you'll set yourself up for an easy par two."

"You should listen to the man," Duke agreed.

Though they couldn't touch ghosts, werewolves could detect spirits. Duke could feel a subtle chill in the air and perceive an unnatural hazy outline where Herbert stood. The spirit's voice was a soft whisper carried by the breeze.

On Earl's next stroke, the ball got trapped in a pocket of ripped felt.

"This can be a tricky one," Herbert consoled. "You fellas don't mind if I play through, do you?"

Duke and Earl granted their permission, and Herbert efficiently scored a hole in one. "It's all physics and geometry. 'Course, I've had a lot of practice." He balanced his ectoplasmic golf ball on the tip of his phantom club. "Y'all have a pleasant evening."

By the fourth hole, it became obvious that the scorecard was completely unnecessary. Duke conquered each green with a single stroke of his rusty putter whereas Earl had yet to sink a single putt before the six stroke limit forced him to move on. His mood steadily worsened even as he protested that miniature golf wasn't even a real sport and that if there were only a bowling alley in town he'd show Duke a thing or two. Duke nodded as if he agreed, but he'd seen Earl bowl.

Earl flipped through the pamphlet as Duke started on hole five.

"Hey! Hey, guys!"

Tammy and Chad stood by the admission shack. She stood on her tiptoes, waving both arms over her head while Chad forked over twelve bucks to Wacky Willie.

"Shit." Earl gritted his teeth. "Just what I need."

Tammy left her boyfriend's side and bounded toward them with a girlish skip. She wore a pleated skirt, a white cotton blouse, and simple black shoes with knee high stockings. At the arc of each skip, the skirt would rise to expose a few inches of her taut thighs. Neither Earl nor Duke could recall what Chad was wearing.

"Hi." Her smile beamed brighter than the course lights.

Earl glanced up from his pamphlet just long enough to nod at her. Duke cleared his throat and spat in a clay pot. "Hey."

She scooted beside Earl. "Remember me?"

"Uh . . . yeah. It's Tanya, right?"

"Tammy, silly." She lightly bopped his shoulder.

Earl sidled away from her.

"So what are you guys doin'?"

"Playin' golf."

She bent over to adjust her stockings. Earl found himself transfixed by her fingers fiddling with that little band of elastic.

"Who's winning?"

Duke's ball rattled in the cup, announcing another hole-in-one.

"We aren't keeping score," Earl replied with a frown.

"Cool."

Chad appeared and handed her a club and ball.

"I got you blue, babe. Just like you like."

"Yeah. Thanks. So, hey I've got an idea. Why don't we join you?"

"We're kind'a in the middle of the game," Earl said.

"So what? I thought you weren't keeping score."

He looked into her eyes and tried to change her mind with a little mesmerism. "You don't want to play with us."

"Sure, we do."

Earl focused his will sharp as a knife. "No, you don't."

"Oh, c'mon. It'll be fun. I promise."

The vampire relented. His powers of hypnotism never were reliable. He didn't practice enough, and whenever he tried, it always gave him a headache.

Tammy brought the full, terrifying force of her dimples and batting eyelashes down upon him. Against such powers, he was helpless.

"Yeah. Sure."

She hopped up and down again, bouncing in all the right ways. "Great."

"Uhmm, can I talk to you a minute, baby?" Chad asked.

Her smile instantly became a scowl that just as quickly turned back into a smile. "Okay."

The teenagers walked away and began a hushed argument.

"Just great," Earl groaned.

"Quit complaining."

"That's easy for you to say."

"Yeah. It's gotta be terrible having a hot seventeen-year-old girl crawling all over you. Boy, am I glad I'm not you."

"It ain't as much fun as it sounds."

"Oh, I'm sure it isn't. As a matter of fact, if I remember right, aren't teenage nymphos part of Dante's sixth circle of Hell?"

Duke chuckled.

"Shut the fuck up."

Earl didn't expect the werewolf to understand. In theory, having an overpowering sexual aura might seem like a perk. In reality, it was just another hassle. He'd learned that the hard way. Not long after becoming undead, he'd discovered the talent. Most people weren't sensitive enough to pick up on it, but when somebody did, especially female somebodies, it was an easy score. He'd catch someone who couldn't take her eyes off him and know he didn't have to do a damn thing to get laid except introduce himself. Sometimes not even that. It was great. For about a month.

Then the drawbacks surfaced. He could never be certain a woman was genuinely interested in him or the vampire in him. Which really wouldn't have made much difference except that not all the women drawn to him were as easy-on-the-eyes as Tammy. And jealous boyfriends and husbands abounded. Earl had been shot, stabbed, dragged nine miles over rough road, and one especially sour husband had even employed a chain saw with admirable skill. None of which had seriously hurt Earl, but few chicks were worth getting run through by a Black & Decker Three-Speed Lumber Master.

Tammy might have been one of them.

She ended the argument with Chad by simply ignoring him. She strode away even as he waved his arms in protest. Chad sneered, but it was clear he didn't have a vote in the matter.

"Who's turn is it?" she asked.

"Ladies first," Earl said.

"That's so sweet. Thanks."

She bent over the tee and wiggled her bottom at him. Or

maybe just in his general direction, he tried to convince himself.

Calling forth the willpower only available to someone who had passed through the veil of death, Earl looked away.

An unpleasant mutter rose from Chad's throat.

The next fourteen holes stretched half-an-hour into twenty years. Earl read his pamphlet and stared into the lights and studied his golf ball until he knew every dimple by heart. He looked anywhere and everywhere Tammy wasn't in a vain effort to discourage her. Somehow, she managed to still fall into his line of vision. It was uncanny how she seemed to be wherever he casually glanced. She gracefully glided to and fro, here and there, bending over this and kneeling beside that and adjusting her stockings and smoothing her skirt to terrifying effect. Admittedly, Earl wasn't putting forth all his efforts in resisting, but the girl knew her body and how to use it. He caught himself staring more than once.

So did Duke. The werewolf's crooked smile never left his face.

Chad made a futile attempt at sticking by his girlfriend's side, but he was constantly outmaneuvered, always one step behind.

The last ball rattled in the last hole, a three-foot-high volcano.

"That was fun," Tammy said. "We'd like to play again, but Chad and me got things to do."

Earl breathed a sigh of relief.

She reached out and touched him for the second time of the evening. It wasn't much. Just a light hand on the small of his back. Enough to send a shudder down his spine to his nether regions.

"See you later," she said.

"Later," Chad agreed through clenched teeth.

The teenage couple returned their equipment to Wacky Willie. Earl and Duke were about to do the same when the ghost of Herbert Smythe appeared by their side.

"Excuse me, but I couldn't help notice you scored a perfect game there, friend."

Duke rolled his golf ball round and round his palm. "Wasn't that hard."

"It's all luck anyway," Earl added.

Herbert ignored him. "Anyway, as you have already probably guessed, I've been condemned to play this course until I score a perfect game. I've mastered all the holes, except number nine, and I was hoping . . ."

"Sure."

"Really. Thanks, I really appreciate this."

"No problem."

Tammy watched the werewolf give the ghost golf tips as the vampire pretended to read his pamphlet while casting regular glances up and down her figure.

Tammy had always assumed that a vampire would be harder to seduce than a regular man. Certainly, a few degrees harder than teenage boys. He wasn't. Earl offered some token resistance, but that was all it was. He was hers whenever she wanted.

She was tremendously disappointed.

Yet she found herself intrigued as well, not by the vampire, but by the werewolf. Duke withstood her flirting assault better than anyone ever had. She caught him watching her from the corners of his eyes several times, but only when she was really looking for it and only, she suspected, because he didn't really care if she caught him.

She wanted him. He was fat and rough, with callused hands and greasy hair, but she wanted him. She'd never wanted anyone before. She gave Chad a jump now and then to keep him in line, but that was a means to an end. She'd let Roger Simpkins get to third base one time, but that was only because he was Denise Calhoun's boyfriend. She'd found Earl interesting until realizing that being an immortal stalker of the night didn't make him any less of a stooge. She'd carried a brief crush on Boris Karloff before discovering he was a puss in real life. But never before had she felt what she felt for the werewolf in the leather jacket.

But by night's end, he would either be dead or driven away. For the briefest of moments, she considered changing her plans, but no amount of wanton teenage lust could sway her from her sacred mission. Which was a terrible pity since she seriously entertained the notion of losing her virginity to him. Chad hardly counted. He was more of a chore than a sexual encounter and a short chore at that.

"You ready to go, babe?" Chad asked.

She nodded.

They climbed onto Chad's motorcycle and peeled out of the parking lot.

THIRTEEN

Once, Make Out Barn had been a haven of teenage activity. Wholly living up to its name, the worn old building played host to regular sessions of heavy petting and awkward groping. There were even one or two acts of genuine sex on the premises, though not nearly as many as locker-room boasts might lead one to believe. The barn was a place for certain people, namely those of surging hormones and acne-induced angst, preferably in groups of two, to get away from the endless hell that teenagers tend to perceive their lives to be until they grow up and realize that real hell generally strikes around middle age, when one discovers that life is either far too short or far too long.

Tammy put an end to that.

Every priestess needed a temple, someplace to practice her forbidden arts in peace and quiet. The first time her mom almost walked in on her as she conjured the spirits had proven that. To that end, Tammy had taken Make Out Barn for her own. It wasn't hard. All it took was some carefully controlled arson and a simple rite of the Dreadful Aura. Her temple had been left alone ever since, making it perfect for her needs. She could study up on her destiny, raise the dead, and leave corpses to soak up black magic without having to worry about kids looking to enjoy the pleasure of swapping various bodily fluids and adults hoping to interrupt such pleasures.

She shone her flashlight on the bodies. The ritual demanded they be buried in shallow graves, and so they sat in inch-deep holes in the ground, covered from head to toe with a thin layer of dirt. The Mark of Those That Inhere Within the Smothering Shadows were carved into their foreheads. The first stage of the magic had taken effect. The fetid flesh of the corpses had become a pallid green, and their teeth had become rows of razor-sharp fangs. Thick, black claws had grown from their fingertips. They were still dead, but soon they would rise to serve her.

Gleefully grinning, she removed the occult odds and ends from her backpack.

Chad shone a light on a dead face. "Uh . . . Tammy?"

She ignored him. Tammy did not exist once she and Chad went through the doors of the temple.

"Mistress Lilith."

"Yes?"

He tiptoed a wide circle around the dead people. "What are we doing with these guys?"

"We?" She chuckled at the pronoun. As if Chad were an equal partner in her destiny. "We are raising the dead."

"Oh. Okay. Like zombies, right?"

"Sort of."

The ritual shared certain elements of zombie-making, but these were a far more dangerous breed of walking dead. The spell itself even entailed some risk to the casters. It was the most difficult feat of black magic she had yet to attempt, and if something went wrong someone would have to be torn apart when her minions first rose. Chad had volunteered for the duty if the necessity arose, though he didn't currently know it.

He reached for the black candle she'd set out. She slapped his hand away.

"Don't touch anything."

"Okay." He cast a nervous glance toward the nearest dead guy. "So do we have to get naked again?"

"No."

"Oh. Are you sure?"

"Yes."

"Oh. Okay."

"Oh, alright," she sighed.

He smiled stupidly as he stripped off his clothes in fifteen seconds flat.

"Your turn, Mistress Lilith."

Chad leered while she got undressed. It wasn't necessary, but it made things easier. Chad would do just about anything as long as they were both naked while doing it.

"You didn't really like that old dude, did'ja, babe?" he asked as he posed and flexed.

"No. Of course not," she replied.

Tammy organized her supplies. There wasn't much to it. She just had to call forth the shadows to enter the corpses which involved a quick incantation. She had Chad lay out his mom's good silverware and her dad's camping tent stakes. She lit the black candle and began. Chad knew enough to sit quietly in the corner while she worked.

"I conjure thee, from the endless night, from the icy hearth of forever quiet, from the shadows which cannot be banished, I conjure thee!"

She put her finger to the page to mark her place and grabbed her pocketknife. After another five minutes of steady incanting, she pricked her index finger.

"Ose-thay at-thay eyeth-wray in-ay arkness-day. Eyes-ray. Eyes-ray. Eyes-ray!"

She flicked a drop of her blood on the black candle. The flame flared, spewing an unnaturally thick cloud. Shapes and things terrible and unknowable slithered in the gray smoke. They whispered and cackled, all too eager to be given form in the world of flesh.

"Eyes-ray!" Tammy shouted. "Eyes-ray and-ay obey-ay eye-may ill-way. Eyes-ray! Eyes-ray!" She threw her arms wide. Her flashlight cast fearsome light across her face. A skittering piece of dark crawled over her eyes.

Chad would have been frozen in sweaty horror had he noticed, but he was too busy staring at her pert breasts as they rose and fell as she incanted.

The smoke funneled downward into the mouths and eyes of the bodies. A chill wind blew. The unholy chattering quieted, and stillness settled on Tammy's temple.

Everything was still quiet ten minutes later.

Chad dared speak up. "Mistress Lilith, is that it?"

She leafed through her *Necronomicon* to find where things had gone awry.

He ventured from the corner and stood by her side. "They're not rising."

"I noticed."

"What went wrong?"

"Shut up, dumbass, and let me think."

He looped an arm around her waist. "I don't know about the dead guys, but I think Big Jimmy is starting to rise."

She was busy deciding which of Chad's body parts to dig her fingernails into when the candle flickered. Five ragged moans rose. Tammy snatched up her flashlight and shone it on the corpses.

Her minions sat up and slowly, clumsily rose to their feet. The four walking dead with two good legs stood in hunched, predatory stances. The fifth one-legged corpse hopped about in an awkward balancing act. Ten sets of beady, milky eyes stared at their new mistress, either awaiting their first command or, perhaps, their first meal.

Chad huddled closer to Tammy, either out of terror or, quite possibly, to cop a cheap feel. Either way, she stomped on his foot to deter him.

She pointed to the door. "Go forth," she whispered. "Go forth and sate your unholy appetites on the flesh of mine enemies."

The corpses shuffled (or hopped) to collect their weapons of knives, salad forks, and camping stakes. They shambled out of the barn one at a time. The last dead thing stopped just long enough to cast a wicked glare at his mistress. And then they were gone.

Tammy raised her hands over her head and giggled the malign giggle of a schoolgirl consorting with the legions of darkness and having a hell of a time doing it.

FOURTEEN

As soon as Duke parked the truck in the diner lot, Earl jumped out, grabbed the battered cassette player from the bed, and started to walk down the road.

"Where you goin'?"

"I'm getting something to eat," Earl answered.

"Any particular reason you're taking the tape player?"

"It's a long walk."

"Don't forget. Sheriff wants a word with you."

"I'll be back in plenty of time."

Earl stepped out of the light of the diner's sign and was swallowed up by the night. He walked about a half-mile down the road before turning around. He wasn't up to the torment Duke would subject him to if the werewolf found out he was going to visit a ghost. He wouldn't say much. Not with words. But Duke could say more with a look than anyone he'd ever met. Earl had seen glass-eating, tough-as-nails, drunken bad-asses retreat in trembling terror at the sight of Duke raising one eyebrow. Earl didn't understand it. He only knew that he wasn't up to the raised eyebrows and knowing half-smiles Duke would throw his way if the werewolf discovered his graveyard date.

"It's not a date," he verbally reminded himself. "It's just a . . ." He searched for a less objectionable noun. ". . . just an appointment."

He frowned. That was a touch too formal.

"Get-together?" he tried, but he didn't like the sound of that either. Not with only two of them getting together.

"Meeting?"

He didn't know what it was, but it was definitely not a date. Cathy was lonely, and he was just being nice. That was all there was to it.

"Rendezvous," he tried, but the word was French enough to carry romantic implications.

"It's just a thing," he quickly decided. "A nice thing. That's all it is."

He skulked up to the graveyard, low to the ground to keep anyone in the diner from spotting him, although he was pretty sure nobody would be watching all that closely. Just to be safe he hopped the broken fence on the graveyard's dark side.

"You came," Cathy said.

She smiled, and, while Earl's body didn't exactly respond like a mortal body, he still felt a strange flutter in his stomach.

"I said I would. I brought this." He held up the dented box. "I thought you might like to listen to some music. 'Cuz, y'know, it's probably been a while since you got the chance." He dug some cassettes out of his overall pockets. "I've got Elvis and Randy Travis, BB King, Buddy Holly—"

"Buddy Holly. That'd be just great."

"You *have* been here a while." He inserted the tape.

"Not that long. I just like Buddy Holly."

Buddy began belting out a static-filled song that wasn't entirely decipherable. Earl fiddled with the knobs to correct the problem, but the crackling remained. He gave up and took a seat beside Cathy on her grave.

"So how was your day?" he asked.

"Same ol', same ol'. I saw some birds. I think they were ducks. And a Volkswagen Beetle drove by. Haven't seen one of those in a while."

"They started making 'em again."

"Cool."

"The engine is in the front now."

She frowned. "Well, that's stupid. It's not really a Beetle then, is it?"

"Nope," he agreed.

They listened to the music a while. She silently sang the lyrics with Buddy.

"How was your day?" she asked.

"Okay. I slept."

"Oh. That's right. I forgot. So do you have to sleep during the day or can you walk around if you want?"

"I'm pretty much dead when the sun's up."

"Do you dream?"

"Vampires don't dream."

"Never?"

"Well, we don't really sleep. We just sort'a shut off."

"Bummer."

Cathy nodded along with the music. Earl considered putting an arm around her shoulder, but it didn't seem right. He wanted to, he thought, but it seemed a little forward on his part. And what if she didn't want his arm around her shoulder? Just because he could touch her didn't necessarily mean she wanted him to.

For just a nice thing, this sure as hell felt like a date. It'd been a long time since he'd been on one, and he'd never been very good at it.

Cathy reached over and took his hand in her own. He was glad the undead didn't have to worry about sweaty palms.

She smiled again. He smiled back again.

"So this cemetery-guardian job," she said, "how does it work? I mean, I can't do anything. How am I supposed to guard anything?"

"I'm not real sure. Have you tried to do anything?"

"Like what?"

"I don't know, but just because you're immaterial doesn't mean you can't do stuff. I knew a ghost in Alabama who could make fog and chain-rattling noises. And there was another in South Dakota that was able to shatter glass and move small stuff around."

"How'd they do that?"

"They just did it. I don't know a lot about ghost powers, but I don't think there is any special trick to it. It's just practice, I think."

Cathy lay back on her plot.

"That stuff about vampires being able to change shape, that isn't true, is it?"

"It's true."

She propped up on her elbows. "No way."

"Sure is."

The ghost grinned with charming suspicion. "You're screwing with my head. There's no way someone . . . even a vampire someone . . . can turn into a bat or wolf."

"And mist," Earl added.

"Yeah, right. It's just impossible."

"Like ghosts and vampires?"

"Okay, smart guy. Show me."

There was teasing doubt in her voice. Coming from anyone else, it would have annoyed him. Coming from her, he could only flash a goofy, lopsided smile.

He bowed. "For my first trick, I'd like to do a little shape-shift I call 'The Wolf.' "

She held her hands out and performed a soft, aristocratic clap.

Like most of his vampiric talents, Earl had never truly mastered shape-shifting. He never had much reason to, and on those few occasions he had, it always left him stiff and sore. Cathy was partly right. Shape-changing was one of the harder feats a vampire might attempt. It involved a lot of bone-shifting, muscle-twisting, and organ-shuffling. Not to mention the displacement of those extra pounds that separated wolf from human. They melted away, but all that nonexistent weight seemed to rest on his kidneys. Or maybe that was just canine instinct that made him want to piss on everything.

He hunched over and balled his hands into tight fists. He grunted and shook with the effort and finally let loose with an embarrassing intestine-churning growl. And nothing happened.

"Are you okay?" Cathy asked.

Earl leaned against a wooden tombstone. "Yeah. Just give me a sec. Getting it started is the hardest part."

He stood tall and straight, attempting to regain some dignity, and tried again. It took a long minute for him to gather together his will and push it through his body. At first it felt like the mother of all bowel movements. The gurgling warm sensation started in his guts and spread from there. Once it started, he just had to ride it out.

His transformation was a lot smoother than Duke's. Whereas the beast within Duke literally burst out of his skin in a gruesome, nausea-inducing metamorphosis, Earl's change was a fluid moment of grace. And, unlike Duke, Earl's clothes even changed with him, disappearing to wherever all his extra weight went. The man melted into the wolf. Not the half-ape monster that Duke became, but an unassuming, feral canine. As a wolf, Earl looked more like a bony mongrel than a wild predator.

Cathy's eyes flashed with delight. "That's fantastic!"

Earl's lips parted and he bared his long, yellow teeth in a canine grin of pride. He took a moment to adjust to his four-legged form and push away the urge to take a leak on all the nearby tombstones.

She reached out and rubbed his muzzle. Then she scratched under his chin. He was tempted to roll over and let her rub his belly, but quickly changed his mind. Naked dogs had a harder time concealing certain biological reactions than fully clothed humans. He let her massage his ears for a few minutes before going into his next trick.

Now that he was back into the swing of things, the change from wolf to bat was surprisingly easy. He flew a couple of quick laps around the graveyard while she watched in wonder. A tremendous satisfaction entered him at the sight of her enjoying herself. It didn't really help her situation, but at least it took her mind off it.

He decided, somewhat optimistically, to try changing to mist. He'd only done it four times before. The last time his concentration had slipped for only an instant, and he'd lost his legs to a sudden gust. But he was willing to lose an appendage or two for another of Cathy's smiles.

It turned out to be easier than his earlier changes. As a cloud of curling fog he drifted in the breeze while concentrating on holding onto all his floating molecules. Cathy passed her ectoplasmic fingers through his body. A tingle ran through his insubstantial nerves. Had he currently possessed knees, they would have wobbled at such an intimate touch. Instead his form of fog tumbled over in an excited, whirling loop. He hoped she didn't notice.

Transforming back into a man proved harder than he remembered. It took considerable time and willpower to gather up all his errant pieces and jell them back into physical form. He wasn't entirely certain, but it felt like some of his internal organs hadn't made the trip back. There was a vague empty sensation where his liver and spleen should have been.

He bowed to another round of applause.

"That's impressive," she observed.

Earl would've shrugged, but his aching shoulder wasn't up to it. A wise vampire always stretched before assuming forms. It was just common sense.

A brown police cruiser pulled into the diner. A tall, lean man Earl guessed to be the sheriff got out and went into the diner.

Buddy launched into a hissing rendition of "Peggy Sue" that sounded as if it were being beamed directly from the outer regions of the galaxy. Cathy jumped up and took Earl's hands.

"This is my favorite. Do you want to dance?"

"I'm not a good dancer."

"That's okay. Neither am I."

"I only know how to waltz."

"Really? Me, too."

Earl glanced at the cruiser. The sheriff could wait another five minutes.

She moved closer, guiding his hand to her back. She began the dance, then smoothly gave him the lead. At first, he was far too busy counting in his head and avoiding open graves to enjoy himself. And though ectoplasm had always been cool to the touch before, something about Cathy made him uncomfortably warm. But gradually, without him even realizing it, she drew closer and laid her head on his shoulder. They slowly spun through the cemetery in each other's arms. They kept dancing even after Buddy was swallowed whole by static.

She smelled like blooming roses and freshly dug earth. Was that the scent of all ectoplasmic beings, he wondered, or was it just her? He'd never gotten this close to a ghost for this long.

"You know, Earl, you were right."

"Yeah? About what?"

"You aren't a good dancer."

"I'm the only one available," he replied with a grin.

"Good point."

He held her at arms' length, and she twirled once. She fell back into his arms.

"Earl, how old are you?"

"Ninety-seven come May."

"You don't look it."

"Well, I try and stay out of the sun. It keeps the wrinkles away."

She laughed. It fluttered through the graveyard, filtering into the world of the living. Any mortals passing by would have stopped and wondered where it came from. They would've found a man dancing with an imaginary partner and decided it better to mind their own business.

Earl and Cathy stopped dancing and looked into each other's eyes. Strands of phantasmal hair drifted across her face in the light breeze. He brushed them away and caressed her cheek. Her blue lips parted ever-so-slightly. They leaned closer.

Earl's heart thumped in his chest. Once. For the first time in sixty-nine undead years.

And then a shadow rose up behind him and plunged a wooden stake through his heart. His eyes glazed, and he crumpled to the ground.

"Earl!"

The shadow crept forward. Cathy could see in darkness better than the living could see in daylight. But she couldn't quite see this creature, an eel of black smoke slithering across the night. In one moment it seemed roughly human-shaped. In another it was a scuttling collection of tendrils. But mostly it was a glob of shifting shadows that refused to be truly perceived by even ghostly eyes.

It didn't seem to notice her. It hunched over Earl in a menacing, amorphous way.

"Get away from him!" Cathy shouted.

The shadow ignored her while running blackened limbs over the vampire.

"I said, get away from him!"

She lashed out without thinking. Much to her surprise, her ephemeral fists connected with a bulb of dark that might have been its head. It squealed and tumbled back. Cathy put herself between Earl and the shadow.

The thing took on an almost human form. Two crimson eyes glinted.

Cathy met its gaze with the lack of fear that came from being dead and the knowledge that there was very little more that could be done to her. So she hoped.

"Back off!"

Something registered in the thing's eyes. It wasn't fear. Perhaps it was respect for a fellow creature of shadow. Maybe regard for her determination. Whatever it was, the shadow decided it didn't want the vampire enough to face her. It slipped away. Cathy suddenly noticed that it was not alone. Four other forms slinked through the graveyard. The five banks of near-imperceptible fog rolled across the road toward the diner. One stepped by the diner's neon sign and became solid under the hard light.

It was a man (or something that had once been a man) with green skin and tattered clothes. It raised its head to the light and hissed. The ravens perched on the sign cawed loudly and flew away. The sign clicked off and, once again, the creature became a shadow swimming in darkness.

Cathy turned to Earl. He wasn't breathing. He wasn't moving. He just lay there, wooden stake poking through his chest, staring up with a blank expression. She didn't know if he was dead, but he'd told her that a stake through the heart wasn't supposed to be fatal. Or was it? She couldn't remember.

"Damn it, Earl. Don't be dead. Please don't be dead."

She turned him on his chest and grasped the stake. It was sticking through the vampire so she could touch it. She pulled. It held tight. She pinned him down with one solid foot on his back and twisted while she yanked. The stake budged. Not much. Barely half-an-inch.

"Come on," she snarled as she tightened her grip and tugged with all her might.

And the ghouls oozed their way toward the diner.

FIFTEEN

Inside Gil's All Night Diner, Duke and Marshall Kopp sat at the counter drinking coffee while Loretta refilled salt and pepper shakers.

"Find where those bodies disappeared to?" Duke asked between sips.

"Found a leg and some tire tracks," Sheriff Kopp replied. "Sent the leg and some photos of the tracks up to White Water for analysis. Fingerprints. Hair fibers. That sort of thing. Probably won't lead to anything, but worth a shot." He drank from his own cup. "How 'bout you? Any progress on your end?"

"We're working on it."

"Well, I'd appreciate if you'd keep me informed on anything you do find out." He checked his watch. "Your friend seems to be running a little late. He wouldn't be trying to avoid me, now, would he?"

"He'll show."

"I guess I'll have to take your word for it being as he's your friend and you know him better than me."

Loretta refilled the sheriff's cup. "You won't get any trouble from the boys, Marshall. They're good fellas."

"I've got no reason to doubt it. Just the same, it'd be nice to meet him. Just to be friendly."

Duke tilted his head and listened. A soft hiss, several soft hisses, fell within his supernatural hearing. He filtered a deep breath through his sensitive nostrils. There was something in the air. Almost too faint for even his senses. It stank of decay, blackest magic, and demons. It was the unmistakable aroma of ghouls.

Every light in the diner flickered.

"Damnation," Loretta cursed.

There wasn't any time for a warning. Duke threw off his leather jacket as the lights snapped off and darkness fell upon the diner. Murky shapes just outside his perception hurled themselves through the front doors. Glass shards spilled across the linoleum with a deafening tinkle. Duke shifted, shredding his clothes. Becoming the beast took bare seconds, but he was in mid-transformation when the shadows pounced upon him.

Sheriff Kopp and Loretta were still coping with the dark. The starry sky cast a weak light through the windows. Just enough to make out the hulking werewolf struggling with shadows.

They oozed and crawled over him. He tried to grab one. It slipped from his grasp like a lump of watery gelatin coated with three layers of grease. It scrambled up his back and roughly shoved a knife between Duke's ribs. The werewolf howled at the touch of silver. The ghoul twisted the blade, thrusting it deeper. Duke yelped. He spun around the darkened diner in a painful convulsion. The ghoul slipped away from him. The werewolf fell to his knees.

The ghouls slithered through the diner, under its tables, over its booths, and across the tile floor. Sheriff Kopp drew his revolver and struggled to draw a bead on the cackling, slippery things. One stood mere feet away. He still couldn't wrap his eyes around it. He couldn't pick out any vital points. What looked like a head one second became an arm after another, then a misshapen foot or possibly a tail.

"Get light," Duke gasped between wheezes.

Loretta ran into the kitchen.

In darkness, ghouls were not wholly real. They dwelt in a semi-material state, just insubstantial enough to make them a pain in the ass yet solid enough to claw, bite, and stab. Duke could barely see the living shades circling around, much less fight them.

He yanked the silverware from his side and squealed like a wounded pup. He tossed the knife away. A ghoulish blob snatched up the blade.

They circled the werewolf, uninterested in the diner's human inhabitants. He leapt on the nearest ghoul. His wicked claws shredded cloth as the shadow slipped underneath him and jabbed him in the thigh with a fork. Another ghoul slid beside him and jammed a knife in his shoulder. He snapped at it. He could taste the rotten flesh on his tongue, but in that fraction of a second it took to close his jaws, they bit into nothing but air. Another blur of darkness whizzed past, slicing Duke's forearm. It was a superficial cut. Barely a scratch really. But it burned like a paper cut doused with fifteen pounds of salt and five gallons of lemon juice. So did the other wounds. It was the silver. It made his blood boil and poisoned his muscles.

The ghouls chuckled dryly. They were playing with him. He wasn't used to being on this end of a fight. He was supposed to be predator, not prey.

The shadows darted around, tearing shallow gashes with each pass. Snarling, he did his best to fend them off, but they easily avoided his claws. Each cut made him slower and weaker. Blood clotted in his black fur and dripped onto the floor. They were mostly flesh wounds. A thousand fiery flesh wounds.

The kitchen doors swung open, and Loretta appeared, brandishing a blazing flashlight in one hand, a shotgun in the other. She aimed the light at Duke. The ghouls became real, solid things. "Good Lord."

The ghouls froze under the sudden brightness. Howling, they covered their eyes.

Sheriff Kopp fired. A ghoul's head jerked, and it fell over only to scramble to its feet. Kopp fired two more rounds into the ghoul's chest. It stumbled back but stayed on its feet. The green-skinned creature hunched over in a predatory stance and tossed an annoyed glance at him. Not angry or upset. Merely bothered, and maybe even slightly amused judging by the grin on its twisted lips.

The ghouls scrambled for the darkened corners of the diner, but one wasn't fast enough. Duke caught it by the leg and dragged it back. It hissed and spat and squirmed as he pinned it to the floor. With relish, he pulled the ghoul's head back. The thin neck cracked. Rotted meat tore. Duke ripped the head off. It glared daggers at him as he threw it aside. The decapitated body kept writhing. Duke wrenched off its limbs, one at a time, in a matter of moments. He broke the torso's spine for added measure. The ghoulish bits still moved. Its head snarled. But a ghoul in pieces was mostly harmless unless someone was stupid enough to stick a toe in its growling mouth.

Loretta swept the diner with her flashlight. Ghouls recoiled from their beams. One creature huddled in a corner. It squinted, shading its eyes, and uttered a low, bestial growl. The flashlight dimmed.

Duke pounced on the ghoul. He seized it by the collar of its moldy suit and raised a clawed hand. The light clicked off. The liquid ghoul seeped through his fingers. Duke sliced at the shadow. It squealed. A piece of black arced through the air, hit the floor, and became a twitching arm. Duke struck again, but the ghoul slipped away.

Loretta fumbled with her broken flashlight, but there was nothing wrong with it. Nothing she could fix. A ghoul rose beside her. She blasted the shadow with both barrels. Somehow, she missed. The ghoul slid underneath her, and hoisted her in the air. It shuddered beneath her tremendous weight and tossed her over the counter. Loretta hit the tile with a monstrous thud.

Kopp turned and fired at point-blank range. The creature didn't try to get out of the way. It just hovered there. But he missed. It fixed him with eyes that were mere pinpoints of red and yellow. Then it moved away, ignoring the mortal in favor of the werewolf.

Duke hunched into a fighting stance as four shadows closed in from all sides. He couldn't take them all. Not with silver and the darkness on their side. Maybe one or, if he was really lucky, two before they decided to stop screwing around and jam a fork in his heart.

The ghouls took on just enough form to allow him to see the grins on their drawn faces.

Duke had always known that it would come down to this. Not this exactly, but a violent death seemed the inevitable end of the curse of lycanthropy. Werewolves didn't die of old age.

The headlights of Sheriff Kopp's police cruiser snapped on. Bright, white light poured through the windows.

Duke bared his teeth in a slobbering smile.

He pounced on a ghoul and sank his fangs in its neck. Flesh and bone tore away. The ghoul's head rolled back, clinging by layers of shredded skin. He snatched the creature's legs. With a feral roar, he yanked, and split the ghoul up to its abdomen. The ghoul growled and twisted in a vain struggle to stand with its mangled body.

Another dead thing with only one leg lurched at Duke. He knocked aside its clumsy charge and shoved his clawed hand through its chest.

The ghouls hissed their call to darkness to extinguish this newest light. Before they could bring their power to bear, the headlights turned off on their own. Only for a spare second. They switched back on again, and the sudden light sent the ghouls into disarray.

While Duke ripped the one-legged ghoul to pieces, the two other walking corpses turned their attention to easier prey. They loped towards Sheriff Kopp with the slow gait of ghouls bathed in light.

Kopp shoved the sixth bullet in his revolver and slapped the cylinder closed. He fired two rounds into its head. The ghoul staggered but didn't fall. Not that Kopp expected it to. He was just hoping to keep it busy long enough for Duke to finish rending his current project. He emptied his gun into the closest ghoul. It jerked and twitched but steadily advanced.

The last two ghouls licked their sneering lips with blackened tongues. Kopp lowered his gun. The weapon seemed useless against them. And the monstrous werewolf creeping up behind them seemed to have everything in hand. A low rumble rolled from Duke's throat, and the walking corpses twirled around to face him.

The next moment was a blur of werewolf savagery and ghoulish shrieks. Even wounded as he was, Duke was more than a match for a pair of ghouls. Even ghouls armed with silverware. As sheriff of Rockwood County, Marshall Kopp had beheld many horrible things, and he had never once turned away. But he turned away now as the ghouls were savaged beneath Duke's glinting claws. Not out of fear or disgust, but to shield himself from all the flying bits. He only turned back after all the screaming had finally quieted. Duke stood over a collection of wiggling body parts.

The diner lights spontaneously clicked back on, revealing the limbs and torsos scattered all around the diner. The legs twitched. The clawed hands drummed their fingers on the floor. The heads rolled around in tight circles looking for a carelessly placed ankle to sink their teeth into.

Kopp holstered his revolver and checked Loretta.

She sat up. "I'm alright, Marshall. Takes more than a little tumble to hurt me." She struggled to get her weight to its feet. "What the hell are these things? They ain't zombies."

"Ghouls," Duke replied. "Part zombie, part living shadow."

"How do you kill 'em?"

"Well, you can burn 'em, but that leaves a stink for days. Or you can wait for the sun and let 'em melt. 'Course, that leaves a hell of a mess."

Loretta frowned. "Not in my diner it won't." She went to the back to retrieve her broom.

Earl walked through the shattered front doors. "Everything okay in here? Jesus, you look like hell, Duke."

The werewolf righted a fallen chair and took a seat. He was a bloody mess, but it wasn't as serious as it looked. Already the gashes were closing. They'd take a few days to heal completely, and, because they were silver inflicted, there would probably be a couple of scars left to remind him of this night.

"Good thinking with the headlights, Earl."

"Thanks."

"You okay?"

The vampire glanced at the hole in his chest. "Oh. This? This is nuthin'. Just a scratch."

Loretta appeared again. Muttering, she swept the dismembered ghouls and broken glass out the door.

SIXTEEN

Tammy gave her ghouls two hours to complete their mission. It was more than enough time, she reckoned. Then she and Chad climbed on his motorcycle and headed out to see the damage her minions had done. She could hardly wait to view the slaughter.

But as the bike neared the diner, Tammy knew something had gone horribly wrong. The lights were on, and a mound of body parts had been piled under the hard neon glow. At first, she'd assumed they were the pieces of those who dared oppose her, stacked there by her minions as an offering to their mistress. Then she noticed their green color, and as Chad pulled into the parking lot, Loretta's hulking shape strode from the diner carrying an aluminum trash can. She dumped the can's contents onto the pile, adding another batch of writhing limbs, snarling heads, and twitching torsos to the mix. Loretta reached into the can and pulled out a handful of innards. She tossed them with the other parts.

"Evening, kids."

Tammy gaped, though not for the reason Loretta would expect.

Loretta wiped her greasy fingers on her apron and went back inside.

Tammy circled the pile. The ghouls averted their eyes and gnashed their teeth in duly embarrassed fashion. This was not how it was supposed to be. Five ghouls, properly armed, were more than a match for a vampire, a werewolf, and one fat waitress. But her minions sat before her, an undulating monument to yet another failure.

"What now?" Chad asked.

Fuming, she grabbed a head and stuffed it into her backpack. She struggled to make it fit, finally settling for holding it closed since she couldn't get the pack to zip up.

"Take me home."

The night was still young, and Chad was still horny. But he knew better than to argue with her when she got like this. She had always been a weird chick doing her weird-chick stuff, but when that tone entered her voice and that darkness rose in her eyes, she got too strange for even him to ignore. At such moments, he could almost feel the malevolent power of her soul, colder than an icicle in his jugular. He sped off to her house, all too eager to get rid of her.

"So . . . uh . . . I'll see you tomorrow," he said.

She jumped off the bike and ran into her house.

"Or something," he sighed.

Tammy dashed into her bedroom. Her dad was engrossed in the middle of a John Wayne movie, and her mom was busy knitting. Her mom was always busy knitting things that nobody ever wore. Scarves, mittens, sweaters, and other pieces of winter clothing that had no purpose in a desert hell like Rockwood.

Tammy shut her door and very quietly locked it. If her father heard the lock turn he would come barreling from the living room and accuse her of smoking dope, or something equally stupid. Then she removed the ghoul head from her backpack and set it on her dresser.

The head hissed. It stuck out its tongue and ran the wrinkled thing round and round its lipless mouth.

"Shut up!" she growled.

The ghoul shot her a squinted glare and opened its mouth as if to howl. She stuffed a sock into the gaping orifice. The head replied with its best sock-muffled cry.

"Mmmpphhh! Mmmpphhh!"

Tammy leaned in close enough that her nose almost touched the open hole where the ghoul's own nose should have been. "Cut it out."

The ghoul lowered its head and nearly rolled onto the floor. It spat out the sock with a frown. The language of ghouls was the language of the abyss. It was a dialect of hisses, growls, grumbles, and other unpleasant noises. Tammy understood it as only a true mistress of darkness could. Just as she was able to read the range of ghoulish expressions which were all subtle variations of scowls and glowers.

"Terribly sorry, mistress," the head apologized, "but I do have an image to keep up. It's not often I'm given form, and I would like to enjoy it while I can."

Tammy sat on the edge of her bed. "What happened?"

"Things got rather mucked up, but it wasn't our fault."

"Who's fault was it then?"

"Since you asked, I dare say, in all honesty, that it was yours, mistress."

Tammy grabbed a pen and stuck it in the ghoul's eye.

"How terribly immature," the ghoul snarled.

"What went wrong?"

"The graveyard guardian. She saved the vampire, who saved the werewolf, who saved the mortals. We weren't prepared for a ghost. And we can't do anything against them anyway. So it really wasn't our fault, now, was it? Can't send ghouls against spirits and expect to win, now, can you?"

"Shut up."

"I was just answering your question, mistress. No reason to get snippy just because you muddled the job."

Tammy rubbed her palms together. "It-shay, uck-fay, amn-day."

The head burst into flame.

"Really, mistress. How infantile."

The ghoul went up like flash paper once alight. Nothing was left but a small pile of ash that she swept into the wastebasket.

She spent the next half-hour listening to music on her headphones and pondering the situation. Everything seemed to be going wrong. She was beginning to question her great destiny. She was a teenager and prone to moments of angst and self-loathing. Whenever such moments hit her, there was only one thing to do. She had to talk to the spirits. She had an easy method of communication in the back of her closet, sitting somewhere behind her checkers and Parcheesi sets. She fished around and removed her Ouija Board.

She'd bought it when first embarking on her occult dabbling and quickly realized how utterly useless it was. Not that it couldn't summon spirits under the right circumstances. Particularly at parties, since the dead were always happy for an invitation to a big shindig. There were so few good parties on the other side. But the kind of ghosts channeled through the board were hardly worth her time. She threw it aside and dug deeper before finally hitting upon the object of her desire: her Magic 8-Ball.

As an instrument of spiritual communication, most Magic 8-Balls weren't much better or much worse than Ouija Boards, but this one was special. It was filled with the blue blood of Goorkamushalavtoteca, Queen of Horrors Unborn. And rather than having to summon a spirit, which was always unreliable, Tammy had already permanently bound a soul into the orb.

She sat cross-legged on her bed, cleared her mind, and shook the spirit awake. Then she explained the situation to the 8-Ball, asked it what to do, and gave it another good shake. She peered into its tiny window and waited for the triangular thingamabob to surface with its reply.

ANSWER UNCLEAR, the ball said.

Tammy rattled the orb once again. It stubbornly held its ground.

ANSWER UNCLEAR.

She gave it a hard smack. The thingamabob dipped below the murky depths and emerged bearing a new message.

PISS OFF.

She rolled the ball in small circles on her bed. The specter in the ball, while invaluable as a source of advice, could be uncooperative at times. Most times, in fact. She couldn't exactly blame him. It had to suck, spending all day in the back of a darkened closet, but it was his own damned fault for pestering her all the time while he'd been free to roam.

"Oh, don't be such a baby. You wouldn't be in this mess if you hadn't screwed up your chance in the first place. You'd be a living god and wouldn't even need me."

The blue blood bubbled and blackened. CRAM IT.

"Alright. If you don't want to help me, I can't really make you. I'll never open the way, but I can deal with that. I'll just graduate, go to California, and become an actress. Anybody can do that."

This was very true. Her abridged *Necronomicon*, being the latest edition, had two dozen rituals on that particular subject. Everything ranging from a three-hour incantation that would guarantee a prime-time sitcom to an elaborate ceremony of human sacrifice that would land a dedicated practitioner a three-picture deal with any major studio.

"It's not my first choice," Tammy admitted to the ghost. "But I'll be just fine. Whereas you'll spend the next five hundred years in a little black ball in a tin box on the bottom of Old Lady Riddler's Well."

She flipped the ball up to read its response.

ALL SIGNS POINT TO NO. The thingamabob dipped and rose again to add, SO GO FUCK YOURSELF.

Tammy abandoned reasoning with the sphere. It usually didn't work anyway. The specter within was possessed of singular stubbornness and determination. He was no ghost of terrible tragedy or unresolved issues. He simply refused to pass into the hereafter because he didn't want to. Few people had the strength of will to fight the pull of final death. But, pigheaded as he was, no one stood between Tammy and her destiny.

Torture was out of the question. Spirits were hard to torment in any effective fashion. So she fell on her last resort: bribery.

"Okay. I'll make you a deal. *Bonanza* is on in ten minutes."

The ball shook. The Cartwrights were his biggest weakness. He'd explained to her once that the Ponderosa was a perfect working model of the hierarchy of the old gods. As she learned more about the secret world, she began to see his point. Once she saw the similarities between Lorne Greene and Tougiauareuadksdel, He Whose Name Cannot Be Spoken and recognized Little Joe as Ahzuulrah, Incarnae of Mad Impulses, everything fell into place. It was almost as if the old gods themselves had subtly reached through the shroud and had a hand in its creation. The specter believed they had. He also believed that the hidden guardians of light had responded by spurring the creation of *Three's Company*. And that the old gods had launched a counterattack in the form of interminable *I Love Lucy* reruns. Back and forth it went. The eternal struggle between light and dark was waged on many fronts. Television syndication was just one of them.

TRY AGAIN, the orb said.

She loathed offering more. She didn't want the specter getting spoiled. But she did really need his help.

"Okay. You can also watch *Charlie's Angels* and *Dukes of Hazzard*. But then it's right back into the closet."

A pair of bright blue eyes appeared in the 8-Ball window before the thingamabob replied, REPEAT YOUR QUESTION. ALL WILL BECOME CLEAR.

SEVENTEEN

Gil's All Night Diner had seen many conflicts. Epic struggles between the living and the dead, roaches and exterminators, asbestos insulation and health inspectors. These clashes, often orgies of wanton violence, paled in comparison to this latest war of wills.

Loretta and Sheriff Kopp locked stares. He stood tall and straight, hands on belt. She folded her thick arms across her large chest. This was no easy feat but served to establish her own unshakable determination. If it came to blows, Kopp wouldn't last long. She outweighed him by at least a hundred pounds. Nonetheless, Kopp held his ground with the courage of a man who had seen sheep explode spontaneously and lived to clean himself up later.

"I'm sorry, Loretta. I'm shutting you down."

She narrowed her eyes to squinty lines buried between her chubby cheeks and wrinkled brow.

"Now I don't want any arguments," he continued. "I told'ja

last time if there was any more trouble, I'd have to do it."

"Damnation," she grunted, opening her frowning lips just enough to spit out the word. "You can't count this little incident. Nobody got hurt."

"Somebody could'a been. I'd hate to think what would'a happened if those two fellas hadn't been here tonight."

"Hell, Marshall, I would'a handled it, regardless."

"And if you couldn't?"

"I would'a."

"Damn it, woman, there's sumthin' wrong with this place, sumthin' evil at work. I'm startin' to think that ol' Gil didn't just wander away. That maybe this business with the diner had sumthin' to do with his disappearance."

"Hell, Marshall, no offense intended to ol' Gil, but he was such a slight fella. He could'a been dragged off by coyotes for all you know. Besides, I can take care of myself."

"And if you can't?"

"I can."

"But if you can't?"

"I can."

He shook his head. "Alright, Loretta. You want to put yourself at risk, that's your choice. But what if there'd been customers tonight. They got a right to expect a meal without risking getting their faces bit off."

"Aw, not that again." She snorted. "Look, that fella wouldn't have lost his nose if he'd been smart enough to leave the zombies to me."

"Be that as it may, I got no choice." Kopp put a hand on her shoulder. "If you insist on keeping this place open, I'm gonna have to arrest you. I don't want to do that, but you know I will."

She winced. "Oh, alright."

"Good. Now don't worry yourself. It won't be permanent. Just till we figure out who's responsible for this. In the meantime, you got someplace to stay?"

"Oh no, Marshall. You can put me out of business, but you can't make me leave. Ain't nobody scarin' me away."

"It isn't safe," he said.

"I ain't goin'."

"It isn't even your property, technically."

"Maybe not legally, but I earned it. And nobody, not zombies or ghouls or even the Devil himself, is gonna run me off."

She adjusted the short tower of tangled blonde hair atop her head and stomped off into the kitchen. Kopp knew that the argument was over. Once Loretta got a notion in her head, nothing was going to change her mind. His only recourse was to throw her in jail. He didn't want to do that. In the course of his career, his jail had seen only a handful of prisoners, mostly disorderly drunks and rowdy passers-through. And, of course, there was Velma Gladstone, who required lock-up every four months when the Gladstone curse hit, and she became a bloodthirsty spider-rat-piranha thing looking to slurp down family pets and lay eggs in their owners. During her fits, Velma could raise quite a ruckus, but something told Kopp that it was nothing compared to the tantrum Loretta would throw behind bars.

Sighing, he went outside. Duke and Earl were leaning on their truck, drinking Cokes and throwing rocks at the mound of ghouls. The scent of death had drawn a mixed flock of ravens, vultures, and owls. They huddled on the diner and its sign, but, so far, seemed put off by the offering of green, wriggling flesh.

Duke had destroyed his last outfit and changed into some of the spare clothes kept in Earl's trunk. The jeans were worn thin, and there were gaping holes in the knees. His tie-dyed T-shirt (size extra, extra large) was still short an extra. The taut cotton fabric held back his gut, looking very much like a dam ready to split open. His favorite hiking boots, now just leather tatters, were replaced by a pair of mismatched, generic-brand sneakers. Earl had yet to change his own clothes, despite the large rip in his shirt and overalls where the stake had been so rudely thrust. The wound was slow in closing, and anyone who cared to look could see a few inches below the flesh.

Sheriff Kopp took a spot beside them on the pickup's fender. "Helluva mess, eh boys? So you sure those things ain't dangerous anymore?"

"Yep," Earl replied.

"And come sunup, they'll melt away?"

"Always do," Duke answered.

The sheriff nodded, more to himself than anyone else. A shrill, feminine voice called from the radio in his cruiser. He moseyed over and reached the receiver through the window.

"Go ahead, Wendy."

The radio responded with a jumbled static reply that neither Earl nor Duke understood.

"Roger that. I'm on my way." Kopp climbed into his cruiser. "Looks like it's one of them nights. The Wilkins ranch is having chupacabra trouble again."

"Sounds like a job for animal control to me," said Earl.

"I'm local dogcatcher, too. Comes with the badge." Kopp climbed into his cruiser. "Guess everything's in hand then. Nice finally meeting you, Earl. What was that last name again?"

"Renfield," Earl said.

Kopp grinned slyly. "You boys planning on staying much longer?"

"Actually—" Earl began.

"We'll be around at least a couple more days," Duke interrupted.

"I'd greatly appreciate it if you'd keep an eye on Loretta. Hate to see anything happen to her just 'cuz she's too stubborn for her own good." He tipped his Stetson. "Have a pleasant evening." He climbed into the cruiser and drove off.

"So you wanna tell me why we aren't getting the hell out of here, Duke?"

The werewolf pitched a rock that struck a green cranium dead center. The head wobbled from its precarious perch atop the mound.

Earl picked up a rock of his own and cocked his arm. He hurled the stone, painfully aware of his semi-girlish throwing style. The projectile arced high and to the right, missing the sizable target by several feet.

"Not that I'm questioning your judgment or nuthin'. Just seems to me that the smarter thing might be to get while the getting's good."

"Can't you feel it, Earl?"

"Feel what?"

"*It.*"

"What *It?*"

"Damn it, Earl. You're undead. You're supposed to be sensitive to this sort'a shit."

The vampire contemplated the swishing half-inch of cola left in his bottle. "What the hell are you talking about?"

"This place. Right here, right now, it's the most important place on Earth."

"Says who?"

"Says every instinct I got. It's like someone is whispering in my ear, speaking to me. Like destiny or fate or sumthin'. And she's telling me not to leave. That leaving right now would be just 'bout the worst thing to do."

Earl smirked. "Give me a fuckin' break."

"You'd hear it, too," the werewolf grunted. "If you'd just listen."

"Yeah, well, I got a little voice in my head, too, Duke. And it's tellin' me that sticking around is just going to get us killed. I already died once. It was a real shitty experience, and that was only halfway. Don't figure the other half to be much more pleasant."

Duke hurled his stone. It careened off the ghoul skull, sending it toppling from the top of the pile. The head snarled as best it was able without a jaw.

"I'm staying, Earl. You wanna go?" He held up the truck keys and jangled them before tossing them on the hood. "I'm getting some sleep. If you're still here in the morning, wake me up. I want to see the ghouls melt." Then he strolled back into the diner.

Earl considered the offer. He could throw his steamer in the bed and take off. He didn't know how far the empty gas tank and the ten bucks in his wallet would get him, but it'd be farther away from here. Maybe not as far as he'd like, but it'd be a start. He could work something out from there. Of course, it was more complicated than that.

Earl counted on Duke to watch him during the day. From sunup to sundown a vampire was vulnerable. Earl had lived with that fact for decades, knowing that every morning he went to sleep he might not wake. Experience told him it was just paranoia. In his whole undead life, he'd never encountered an actual vampire hunter. There weren't any as far as he knew. Rumors filled vampire society, such as it was, and whenever two bloodsuckers met, one of them always had a scary story to tell. It always involved a friend of a friend of a friend of a guy that knew a friend of theirs who woke up with his head lopped off. The boogeyman of the undead, Earl knew, that was all the hunters were. Just the same, he liked his head connected to his neck, and he liked having Duke watching his back. Just in case.

Beside that, there was the whispering. Earl had heard it, too, though he was loathe to admit it. Probably louder and more clearly than Duke did. The diner did call to him. Or something inside it. It was a dark slithering thing crawling around in his ears that grew stronger each day. It repulsed him, but if he ran away now something horrible would happen.

And then there was Cathy. The idea of leaving her behind bothered him more than anything else. His dilemma would be a lot easier if he could just ask her to go with him. Just his luck to develop feelings for a ghost anchored to a two-acre plot of land.

He found one more good rock, and tossed it with all his might. He released too late. It bounced off the gravel lot and skipped to within a few inches of the ghoul pile. The green corpses chuckled dryly.

"Goddamn," he muttered.

He shoved the keys into his pocket and headed for the graveyard.

EIGHTEEN

As the first rays of dawn spread across the desert, the ghouls put an end to their ceaseless raspy chattering and fell silent. Legs flopped around in the air in a vain attempt to run for cover. Detached arms twisted to cover their squinting yellow eyes. They squealed in the ghoulish tongue.

"Bugger, I hate this part."

"Well, no point in complaining," another ghoul replied.

"True, true," a head agreed somewhere from the center of the pile.

"Mooof glu tlak," a jawless head seconded.

"See you gents on the other side."

"Any plans?" the head atop the pile asked.

"Oh, nothing much," the buried ghoul replied. "Just float around in the sullen ether. Wait to be called upon again. Review my performance this go-around."

"I thought you did a marvelous snarl."

The ghoul would have blushed had his dead flesh been able.

"Perhaps, but I found your scampering quite sinister. And I wish I had your talent for hissing."

"You're too kind, but really, anybody can hiss. Now that bit of shrieking you did when the werewolf tore you apart, that was genius."

"Gluf fof wukal."

"You flatter me."

"I hear there's a cult in Paris with several openings. What say we float over there and give it a look-see?"

"I don't know about that. Can't say I particularly care for the French."

"Now, now, we fleshless ones can't afford to be choosy."

"Gluf fug gok ruffil."

"Excellent point, fellows."

"Oh, here it comes."

And then the sun poked its way over the horizon, and the melting began. Green flesh liquefied. Eyes oozed from their sockets. Foaming bubbles boiled and burst in loud, popping splatters. The ghouls shrieked their death rattles. Not that any of it was all that painful for things that were already dead, but they were determined to enjoy their last remaining moments of form with a good screeching contest. The goo of their flesh slid off their bones, settling in a thick green paste beneath skeletal remnants. The bones blackened and cracked. The bare skulls uttered one last groan before crumbling into gray dust. The bone dust and the fleshly muck mixed into a putrid syrup that smelled of rotten apples and fresh cow dung.

Loretta pinched her nose. "Damnation, that's a stench. I thought you said they stank when you burnt 'em."

"They stink when you let 'em melt, too. Just not as much."

Loretta went inside and returned with a length of green hose wrapped under her arm. She screwed it into the faucet in the diner's side.

"I appreciate you boys staying around, but you don't need to do it on my account. I can take care of myself just fine."

"Ain't about you. Whoever sent these things here, sent 'em to kill me and Earl. You, too, but mostly us. That makes it personal."

Loretta turned the faucet handle. The spigot groaned, gurgled, then shuddered to life with a loud grinding clatter. She sprayed the slime. It refused to dilute or even break apart, but she managed to push it from the lot into the tall, yellow grass where it stayed hidden reasonably well. A trail of brackish greenish gray runoff was left behind.

"If we're gonna figure this thing out," Duke said, "it's time we stopped waiting around for stuff to happen."

"What do you want me to do?" Loretta asked.

"I need you to check around town. You gotta find out everything about this plot of land. How long this diner has been here. What it was before it was a diner. Any odd history."

"There's a hall of records in Leeburn. And Biff Montoya has a collection of every copy of the *Rockwood Examiner*. Went out of business three years ago but might have sumthin'."

"Good. And ask around, too. Anybody who might know sumthin' important. In the meanwhile, I'm gonna check this place out top to bottom."

"Lookin' for what?"

"Don't know yet. Anything unusual."

"I already did that when I first opened it back up. I didn't find nuthin'."

"Maybe you didn't know what to look for."

"Well, I was just mainly looking for rats," she admitted. "Didn't think to check for signs of the Devil. Though, come to think of it, there was a loaf of moldy bread that looked to have fallen out of the Lord's good graces." She shuddered at the remembrance.

Duke went back to bed for a few hours before beginning his inspection. By then, Loretta had taken off on her research quest, and he was left by himself in the bunker of concrete unless one counted Earl curled up in his trunk. Duke didn't. The vampire was far more dead and much less undead during the day. Far better company, by Duke's reckoning, but about as useful as a hundred-thirty-eight-pound sack of flour.

Duke began in the kitchen. He was busy digging through the cabinets when his hearing picked up the squeak of sneakers against tile.

Someone called from the front. "Hello? Anyone here?"

He recognized the voice and went to the rectangular window that allowed one to see into the dining area. Tammy stood by the counter. She smiled upon seeing him.

"Earl's not here," he said.

"Oh. Well, I'm not here to see him."

"Loretta ain't here either."

"Oh. So you're all alone. By yourself?"

"Yeah, and I'm kinda busy at the moment."

"Okay. Say no more. I understand."

"Thanks."

Duke went back to sorting through the kitchen's contents. He didn't hear Tammy leave but assumed that was due to the clatter of pots and pans. He quickly learned otherwise. The nubile teenager pushed open the swinging kitchen doors.

"What'cha doin'?"

"Just cleaning things up," he replied.

"Need some help?"

"Thanks, but I got it."

"Don't be silly. I don't mind."

"Fine. You wanna empty that cupboard for me?"

"Sure." She began transferring canned goods to the counter. "So what happened last night?"

"Ghouls."

"Really? Wow. Is that how you got that cut?"

Duke felt the tender pink slash on his neck. "Yeah."

"Was anybody hurt?"

"Nope."

And the questions continued. Tammy proved an efficient helper, but she subjected him to an endless stream of inquiries and comments on topics ranging from bands to movies to boys and favorite foods. Duke, never much for small talk, replied with curt "yes's," "no's," or whenever possible nods or shakes of his head. By the time they finished with the kitchen, he knew more about Tammy than he really cared to.

"Don't you have school today?" he finally asked, his patience wearing thin.

"I cut." She put fingers to her lips. "You aren't going to turn me in, are you?"

Duke half-smiled, despite himself. She had a way about her that made it hard to get annoyed. Even when he managed to work up some irritation, she'd bat her eyelashes or smile or laugh, and every ounce of annoyance would dissolve.

"You want to help me board up the front doors?"

"Sure."

She held the planks in place while he hammered in the nails. After they'd finished, they took a break. They sat at a table, drinking sodas.

"You know, you've got great hands." She reached across the table and grabbed one of his hands. Her own diminutive fingers traced the deep creases in his palm. "Your skin's so rough, like leather. And this scar gives you real character."

She pointed to a subtle scar just beneath the flesh. It was the Sign of the Pentagram, Mark of the Beast. It grew more or less prominent depending on the phase of the moon, but it never went completely away.

"How'd you get it?" she asked.

"Long story."

"Aw c'mon. You can tell me."

"Ran over a werewolf."

"Yeah, right."

"God's honest truth."

He never bothered lying about the scar. Not that many people asked about it. But of those that did, none ever believed him anyway. Coming up with a story, even a rudimentary one, seemed a waste of time and effort.

She grinned. "Even a man who's pure of heart and says his prayers by night . . ."

"I hate that movie," Duke said.

"What about *An American Werewolf in London*? You gotta like that one."

"S'alright."

She leaned closer. The neck of her T-shirt opened to reveal a tantalizing glimpse of the spot between her cleavage. "So what movie do you like?"

"*Young Frankenstein*"

He pulled his hand from her gentle touch. It wasn't easy, but being a werewolf had taught him the virtues of self-control.

"Duke, do you think I'm pretty?"

He didn't bother lying. She already knew the answer.

"Yeah."

She twirled a strand of her black hair around a finger. "You wanna make out?"

He was not surprised by the question. She was throwing off a mating scent he could smell from a mile away.

"No, thanks. I better get back to work."

He pushed away from the table and went into the back.

Tammy was too astonished to follow. No one had ever turned her down. Not that she'd asked many. Just Chad, and Denise Calhoun's boyfriend, and her physics teacher. The teacher had resisted at first, but he'd succumbed quickly enough. She had always known, always taken it for granted, she could have anyone she wanted. But the werewolf spurned her. The entire concept boggled her so that, even after seeing it, she could not believe it had happened. And yet, the rejection was not an all-together unpleasant feeling. It excited her to realize that seducing Duke would be a challenge.

And she so relished a challenge.

NINETEEN

Earl awoke with a craving for coffee.

The physiology of the undead was such that caffeine, like most any other foreign substance, did nothing to vampires. He could drink a gallon of arsenic or pop cyanide tablets all day long with no ill effects. He'd been bitten by rattlesnakes and swallowed Liquid-Plumr on a dare without even getting nauseous. Eating garlic soup made him break out in itchy, pus-filled sores, but barring that one exception, there wasn't a drug or food on this earth that could bother him to any noticeable degree. It had seemed a good thing at first, but, like most gifts of eternal life, it came at a high price.

He couldn't get drunk anymore. He still drank, but it was only a lingering habit from his breathing days. Much as he might like to drown his sorrows in a night of alcohol-induced debauchery, it just wasn't possible. Such simple pleasures were sadly denied the undead. That didn't mean he didn't still give it a try every now and then. He'd always entertained the notion that there was a brand of beer out there, somewhere, that would do the trick. His holy quest for it had yet to yield anything worthwhile, but he refused to give up. Even if it took a thousand years, he would find it.

In the meantime, he really needed a cup of strong black coffee this evening. The desire was purely psychological. Just the same, when the thirst for a hot cup of joe hit, it was every bit as compelling as his vampire craving for blood. Even more so.

Which only made it all the more unsettling when he dragged himself into the kitchen to find it politely ransacked. Cans and boxes strewn about in neat gatherings on the counter, pots and pans littering the floor. Somewhere amidst the clutter were the various odds and ends of an unassembled cup of coffee. His mood had worsened by the time he found them all.

He shuffled out of the kitchen. Loretta sat at a table covered with newspapers.

"Evening, Earl."

The vampire grunted and went to the coffee machine. He set it to its sacred task, leering at the blinking lights the whole while. When it finally spit out enough for a small cup, he hastily poured it into a dirty mug that he'd found somewhere along the way from his trunk to the machine. He gulped down the piping hot elixir. It seared his tongue and throat raw. Third degree burns regenerated in seconds. Even if they didn't, the pain was worth it.

"Loretta," he said while the tip of his tongue was still crispy. "Where's Duke?"

"Elmyra Werner havin' some problem with her chickens. She asked Duke if he wouldn't mind taking a look."

Earl poured another cup. "What sorts of problems?"

"They ain't dead or nuthin'. Said she'd checked on that after hearing about Walt's cows."

The vampire strolled over to the table and had a seat. He picked up a yellowed newspaper. "What's all this for?"

"Research. On the diner."

"Anything interesting?"

"Kind'a hard to tell."

The placebo effect of the caffeine had yet to fully kick in, but Earl picked up a paper anyway with mild interest. He perused the whole thing. It didn't take long. It was only three pages, and most of that was editorials, weather reports, and a word jumble. He glanced through another paper after that. And a quick scan of a third revealed Loretta's problem.

Rockwood had a rich and colorful history of the unnatural. Every edition of the *Rockwood Examiner* had something along those lines. Everything from rivers of blood and cow mutilations to more unconventional phenomena such as the day all the cats in town lost their tails or the night that lasted three weeks. Corpses disappeared from their graves with fair regularity. Mysterious deaths were not uncommon. And, judging from the number of reports, every third house had to be haunted. The moon did something odd at least every couple of months: either becoming full out of its phase, or changing color, or once, disappearing altogether for an entire week. Unfettered by the laws of normality, the unnatural ran rampant in Rockwood County. It made it hard to pin down any particular pattern.

Earl finished reading an editorial debating on the civil rights of the restless dead and whether blowing off their heads was a violation of these theoretical rights. Interesting points were

made on each side. The pro-rights opinion was that dead people were still people and still endowed with certain basic rights
according to the Constitution. The con argument went along
the lines that someone, living or dead, forfeits most their
rights when they start gnawing on your limbs.

Earl set the paper aside and went for his third cup of coffee.
"You got a map of town?"

"Think I got one somewhere. Want me to get it?"

He nodded while filling his cup to the top.

Loretta found her map, a simple rendering by a local map-
maker several years out of date. She spread the crumpled paper across the table, smoothing out the wrinkles.

"Will this do?"

He sipped from his steaming mug. "Should. You got any
thumbtacks?"

"What for?"

"So we can mark the map."

"Can't we just use a marker?"

He shrugged. "Don't see why not. It's your map."

She removed a pen from her pocket and tapped it on the
table. "What do you got in mind here?"

"We go through these papers and mark every point of re-
ported activity, year by year. Maybe they'll show some sort of
pattern we just aren't seeing."

"That's not a half-bad idea."

"Saw it in a movie once. There was this serial killer running
around, and the police detective, he puts this big map on the
wall and puts pushpins in each of the murders and reckons the
killer's writing out a sign of the zodiac. Capricorn or Cancer or
sumthin'. Once he figures that out, he's able to track down the

killer and stop him from killing the next victim, who just happens to be the cop's girlfriend. Cop shoots the killer just in time, but 'course he ain't dead the first time. He gets up when nobody's looking, even though he's got six bullets in him, and the girlfriend ends up having to shoot him a coupl'a more times."

"I think I saw that one."

"*Blood Hunt* or *Dark Blood* or *Blood Stalker*," Earl recalled. "Sumthin' with blood in it. Anyway, it worked in the movie. Might work here."

"Worth a shot," Loretta agreed.

Earl started with the most recent edition of the *Examiner* and worked his way backwards. He read off the relevant articles while Loretta marked the map. She scribbled the year in small circles. Forty-five minutes later, a pattern was indeed evident. They were in the middle of deciphering it when Duke showed up.

"How were the chickens?" Earl asked.

"They just needed some better feed." Duke pulled up a chair and picked up a newspaper.

Earl pointed to the map. "Look here. There's a steady increase in phenomena each year. Not a whole lot. Just a small rise every year."

"Yeah, so?"

"So, if you go back far enough, you'll see that 'bout eighteen years ago, there was a huge jump. There's still stuff going on before that, but not near as much. And it's not as powerful either. Goes from poltergeists and crop circles to zombie outbreaks and massive rodent migrations." He snapped his fingers. "Just like that."

Loretta screwed up her face in a quizzical expression.

"You're right. Funny. I've lived here all my life, and I never noticed that."

Duke spoke up from behind his paper. "Likely you wouldn't. It's like watching water heat up. Don't really notice until it's boiling. And whatever caused the rise probably made it seem perfectly normal."

"It messed with my head?"

"Messed with everybody's head."

"Don't think I like that much." She snarled. "Nope, can't say I care for it at all. Feels like I've been, well, I don't know, like I've been violated."

"It's just your mind," Earl said. "Not like someone poked out your eyes or broke your fingers."

"Guess so."

"Anyway," Earl continued, "there's gotta be sumthin' that happened eighteen years ago that made this happen."

"How do we figure out what it was?"

"Look through the papers again, I guess."

"Don't think that'll be necessary." Duke held up the *Examiner* he was reading for them to see. "Eighteen years ago, fifteenth of March." He jabbed his finger in a human interest story in the corner.

GIL WILSON OPENS ALL-NIGHT DINER. A grainy black-and-white photograph of Wilson sat under the line. He was a small, unremarkable man. As indistinct and bland as his restaurant.

Loretta snatched the paper from Duke's hands. "Damnation. How can you be sure it ain't just a coincidence?"

Earl marked the map where the diner stood. The big, black X sat in the rough center of a circle of supernatural activity extending fifty miles in every direction.

"Maybe it's just a coincidence?" Loretta said.

"Hector has a rule 'bout coincidences," Duke replied. "One don't mean much. Two means the universe is trying to tell you something. Could be we're sitting in another St. Louis Arch."

"Maybe," Earl agreed.

"The arch isn't just a landmark," Duke explained to Loretta. "It's a transdimensional portal. 'Least, that's what it was supposed to be. Some demons were plannin' on opening a door to Hell with it."

"Not Hell," Earl corrected. "Purgatory."

"Same difference. Didn't work anyway."

"And Big Ben ain't just a big clock. It's actually the Stopwatch of Infinity. Some mystics put it together to keep the world from ending. There's a cog in there that literally carries the fate of the world."

"Don't forget about the Great Pyramids," Duke reminded.

"What about them?" Loretta couldn't resist asking.

Earl leaned in closer. "Turns out they really were landing pads for ancient astronauts."

Her left eye widened in astonishment while the right narrowed suspiciously. "You're kiddin'."

The vampire couldn't hold back his chuckle any longer. "You're right. I'm lying. The pyramids are just giant Egyptian tombstones. But the rest is all true." He raised a hand, palm forward. "Bloodsucker's honor."

"Point is," Duke said, "just 'cuz this place looks like a diner, don't mean it's just a diner. The Chinese believe places can channel the power of the Earth."

"Fung shee," Earl said.

"Fong si," Duke corrected.

"Fing chu."

"Fung soy."

"Whatever you call it, if Gil Wilson knew the right way to put this diner up it could amplify the weirdness factor this particular spot throws out."

"Now that I think about it," Loretta mused, "it does seem kind'a odd that somebody would build a diner this size this far from the highway. So you're saying Gil wanted this to happen?"

"He wanted sumthin'. The supernatural jump might have just been a side effect. Guess the best thing to do now would be to take Polaroids of the whole place, top to bottom, and send it off to Hector. He might be able to spot sumthin' we missed."

"And you think that'll help us figure out why someone wants me out of here so bad?"

"No guarantees, but it's a start."

Loretta went off in search of her camera.

Earl poured his fourth cup of coffee of the evening. It'd get him jittery, but at least he didn't have to worry about being kept awake all day.

TWENTY

Earl ducked out of the diner under the pretense of getting something to eat, but he wasn't hungry. Not hungry enough to bite into a cow's neck. He wanted to make a phone call. The phone at the diner was dangerous to use. He didn't want Duke overhearing it, and given the werewolf's hearing, a mile or two was just playing it safe.

Earl found a pay phone sitting beside a decayed, long-forgotten gas station. Naturally, the station was haunted by a pair of ghosts: one chubby guy in ectoplasmic overalls covered in ectoplasmic grease, and a Scottish terrier. Earl reckoned there had to be as many spirits living in Rockwood as people. Maybe more. The attendant ghost slumbered on a bench beside the broken-down pumps while the terrier trotted over to the vampire.

Normally he'd just ignore the mutt, but his feelings toward restless spirits had changed over the last couple of days. He petted the terrier for a few minutes before making his call. It had to be collect, but he knew Hector wouldn't mind.

"Hec, yeah it's me. Yeah, we still got problems with the diner, but I got sumthin' else to ask."

The spirit dog began to sniff his ankles just a little too aggressively. He nudged it away, but it was not so easily discouraged.

"Is there any way to loose a graveyard guardian?"

While Hector explained the ins and outs of spiritual emancipation and Earl took notes, the terrier mounted his leg and went to town. Earl shook and kicked, but it held fast, clinging with a supernatural tenacity unavailable to dogs of flesh and blood. Earl finally decided it was easier to let it finish up. He thanked Hector for his help and headed toward the graveyard. The dog followed.

On the way, Earl spotted a cow and decided to grab a meal of convenience. If he didn't get something tonight, he'd just have to force himself to do it tomorrow. He was in the middle of climbing the fence when the terrier dashed forward and started barking at his supper. The dog nipped, sinking immaterial teeth into the bovine's ankles. The cow, being a simpleminded creature unable to logically deny the existence of ghosts, awoke and trotted off. The terrier returned to Earl's side. Its eyes shone with canine pride.

Earl hopped off the fence. "Yeah. Great job there, boy."

The dog's tail wagged so quickly it blurred into ectoplasmic mist.

Back at the graveyard, Earl couldn't wait to tell Cathy the good news. She smiled wide with his arrival and held out her open arms.

"Napoleon!"

The terrier jumped into her arms and licked her face.

Her voice raised a squeaky octave, and her lips puckered up in an absurd expression. "How's my favorite boy? How's my favorite boy? Has he been good?"

"He's been swell," Earl replied.

She made some ridiculous kissing noises at the mutt, who licked her some more to make sure every inch of her face was covered in slobber. She set down Napoleon. The dog went off to investigate the many open graves.

"Isn't he cute?"

"Real sweetheart." Earl tried to sound like he meant it.

"He's been my only company since I was buried. Comes by every so often to say hi."

"Great. Napoleon, huh?"

"That's the name I gave him. I don't know his real name. Do you like it?"

He leaned against a loose tombstone. It shifted under his weight. "Good a name as any."

She sat beside him. The tombstone didn't notice. "So did everything work out okay last night?"

"Nobody got killed." He held up his notepad and quickly changed the topic. "I think I can get you out of this cemetery."

"Really?"

"Maybe," he said. "It's a pretty basic piece of magic according to a friend of mine, but I'll have to round up some supplies first. If it works, you'll be able to leave the graveyard whenever you want."

"Cool. I guess."

"What's wrong?"

"Well, I'll still be dead, won't I?"

He nodded.

"So where could I go that would be any different than this? I mean, a change of scenery would be nice, and I appreciate the effort. But, still, what would I do? Where would I go?"

Earl swallowed a deep breath.

"You could always go with me." There was a shudder in his voice he hoped she didn't notice. "I mean, if you wanted to."

"Really?"

"Why not?"

"And Napoleon. Can he come with us, too?"

The ghost terrier raised his head and yipped.

Earl didn't relish the idea of nightly phantom ankle rides. But he couldn't say no to Cathy about anything. If she'd asked him to stay and watch the sunrise, he'd have readily agreed.

"Okay."

She threw her arms around him. Earl unconsciously pulled away. The shifting weight uprooted the tombstone, and they fell to the ground. He wound up on his back with Cathy lying half on top of him. The weight of spirits was practically non-existent, yet she pressed down on him like a two-ton safe. He felt short of breath, which didn't make a whole lot of sense considering the undead didn't need to breathe. They laughed. She started first, and he followed along. He put a hand on her shoulder to help lift her away but ended up drawing her closer.

Then they were kissing. A warm, lingering kiss that lasted forever yet not nearly long enough. He'd never kissed a ghost before. It wasn't much different than kissing a living person except for a slight taste left on his lips. A taste of roses and morning dew and, strangely, Dr. Pepper.

She smiled. "Wow."

He was completely aware of the stupid, lopsided grin across his face. He didn't care.

"That was . . . nice," Cathy said.

"Yeah." His grin grew stupider and more lopsided. His mouth nearly fell off his face. "Nice."

Napoleon barked.

There was the unmistakable wet pop of a beer can being opened. Earl glanced over Cathy's shoulder. Duke stood mere feet away.

"Earl," the werewolf greeted. "You wanna introduce me to your friend?"

"Shit," the vampire grunted.

Cathy jumped to her feet. She beamed enthusiastically and held out a hand. As a ghost, she so rarely got to meet new people.

"Hi! I'm Cathy!"

He didn't take her up on the handshake.

"He can't touch you." Earl sat up. "He's a werewolf. Not a vampire."

"A wolfman. Really?"

"Werewolf," Duke corrected. "Wolfman is some dork with a facial hair problem runnin' through Transylvania, mugging Gypsies."

"Oh. Sorry." She ran her fingers through her hair with an embarrassed grin.

"S'alright."

Duke snapped off a can of Old Milwaukee from the six-pack under his arm and tossed it through Cathy's insubstantial form. Earl fumbled his catch. It bounced off his knee and rolled in the dirt.

"I thought you gave up drinkin'."

Duke sucked down the beer and crushed the can. "It's just a coupl'a beers." He tossed the empty aside and opened another.

Earl wiped the dirt off his own beer. "Cathy, this is Duke. He's a friend of mine."

"So you're really a werewolf?"

"Yup."

"And you guys are really friends?"

"Sort'a," Earl replied hesitantly.

"That's cool. I always thought werewolves and vampires didn't get along." She chuckled. "Well, I never thought vampires and werewolves really existed before. Even after I died, I never gave it much thought. But I figured just because ghosts existed that wasn't necessarily proof that other . . . uh . . . things existed."

She grinned.

"Sorry. I'm babbling, aren't I? I'm just not used to having so much company. What I meant to say was that I'd always just assumed that vampires and werewolves didn't get along. I don't know why, but I always got that impression."

"It's a common misconception," Earl said.

Duke's affinity with animals extended to even deceased, incorporeal dogs. Napoleon found his way by the werewolf's side. The terrier stared up with eager eyes. Since petting was impossible, he was just happy to be near Duke.

The werewolf bent on one knee and dangled his fingers over Napoleon. The terrier snapped at the digits playfully.

Cathy glided over and looped her arm around Earl's own. For the first time ever, she made him uncomfortable. Actually she made him uncomfortable all the time, but this was the first time she did so in a bad way. It wasn't her fault. It was Duke's.

The werewolf just kept looking at him in that annoying, I-know-more-than-you way of his. Duke didn't talk much, but Earl knew what he was thinking. Most times. Occasionally Duke would cast a glance that defied interpretation. During those cryptic moments, Earl knew Duke had figured out some ultimate secret of the universe that he wasn't quite willing to share with anybody else.

He was giving Earl one of those looks now, made all the more irritating since Duke wasn't even looking directly at him. Just playing with the ghost dog, acting like he wasn't thinking what he was.

"Duke, can I talk to you for a second?"

The vampire tried to smile politely and ended up scowling instead. "In private."

"No problem."

"Would you excuse us for a moment?" He squeezed Cathy's hand and let go reluctantly. "I'll be right back."

"It was nice meeting you, Duke."

Duke bobbed his head back at her. "See you around."

Earl led him through the graveyard gates and into the middle of the dirt road. He plastered a fake smile across his face for Cathy's benefit.

"How'd you know where to find me?" Earl asked.

"Wasn't hard. Diner's just across the road there. And last night, you came in reeking of ectoplasm."

"Damn." Earl had forgotten Duke's powerful nose was sensitive enough to smell even the stuff of spirits.

"Goddamn it, you prick. How long were you standing there?"

"Long enough. So you like this girl?"

"Yeah. Yeah, I like her. Okay, I like her. Is that alright with you?"

Duke's reply was a slight, hardly noticeable smirk.

Earl's toothy smile grew wider as his exasperation rose. "And you know what? She likes me. That's right. *Me*. You got a problem with that?"

"Nope."

They stood in silence for a few seconds. Finally Earl couldn't take it anymore.

"You asshole. Why do you got to do this to me?"

"I ain't doin' nuthin' to you."

Earl threw up his hands. "The hell you ain't."

"Careful there, Earl. Your girlfriend's watchin'."

Cathy stood at the edge of the cemetery. She smiled and waved at the vampire. Earl smiled back.

"I know what you're thinking, Duke. You're thinking I'm fooling myself. That a girl like that is too good for me. That if she wasn't a ghost and I wasn't a bloodsucker she'd have nuthin' to do with me."

"Is that what I'm thinkin'?"

"Yeah. And you know what, you fat son of a bitch? You're right. And you know what else? I don't care. She likes me. I like her. And she's coming with us. You got a problem with that?"

Earl intensely glared into Duke's chin. He would have looked into his eyes, but resorting to an upward angle would've been admitting the werewolf's size advantage. Of course, size was just one of his advantages. If the impulse hit him, he could easily rip off Earl's right arm and shove it down the vampire's throat. Earl hoped he wouldn't. Not while Cathy was watching.

"Earl, you dipshit."

Duke slapped Earl on the shoulder. Earl stumbled, nearly tumbling over. The werewolf grinned an actual, honest-to-God, wide smile. Earl had never seen Duke do that before. He didn't even know it was possible. He'd always assumed Duke didn't have the necessary muscles for such expressions.

Duke chortled, tossed a wave to Cathy, and headed toward the diner. Napoleon trotted after him. Just before he went back inside, he turned back, wearing one of his regular, understated smiles.

He'd figured out another of those Goddamn secrets.

Earl felt almost close to getting this one himself, but rather than spend any more time pondering it, he just headed back to the graveyard.

TWENTY-ONE

Tammy's parents let Chad come over to the house for regular tutoring sessions. Despite her unexceptional grades, it was a plausible reason: Chad's grades were even worse. Her parents even let them be alone in her room as long as the door was open a crack.

Very little tutoring went on in Tammy's room. Depending on how educational someone might consider Chad copying Tammy's homework. He sat at her desk and busily copied her history homework while Tammy flipped through the latest edition of Crazy Ctharl's Hard-To-Find Sorcerous Emporium. The catalogue was a necessity for the modern high priestess. In the Dark Ages, finding fresh mandrake root or the spleen of a virgin wasn't all that hard. In the twentieth century, who had the time to dig around beneath a hangman's tree or figure out what a spleen even looked like. Crazy Ctharl's catalogue was a lifesaver. It offered reliable delivery, though it didn't use the mail. Somehow, whatever you ordered found its way to you. Usually wrapped in discreet brown paper. Though there was that time Tammy ordered a bag of Hitler's ashes and found it under her pillow before she'd even sent in the order.

Best of all, the prices were reasonable. She was on a tight budget and finding the glittering scales of Hecate for only three dollars a pound made things so much easier. The cover boasted "Prices so low, you'll question the collective dream of sanity." Beneath that, another line declared, "The darkness approaches, and Ctharl says everything must be sold before the Lords of Doom swallow the world!" Crazy Ctharl always said the world was ending. This once, he was right.

Tammy skimmed through the pages. There were lots of things she wanted. The fang of a shadow, candles made with the Wax of Vorgo, and a wide assortment of sacrificial daggers. She didn't let these items distract her. She stuck with only what she needed. Her savings still fell short. She marked off the items she could scrape together with a little effort on her part, and still needed a few more dollars.

"How much money do you got, Chad?"

Chad stopped copying. "What?"

"Money," she sighed. "How much do you have?"

He reached into his pockets and pulled out a couple of bucks.

"Not on you, stupid. I mean, how much do you have saved?"

"My grandma gave me a hundred bucks for my birthday, but I'm saving it for a trip."

"I'll need it."

"But I'm saving it for a trip," he whined, in case she hadn't heard him the first time.

Normally, she would have called upon her feminine wiles to

persuade him. She wasn't in the mood. She frowned and squinted hard in his direction.

Chad went back to copying. Even with his back to her, he could feel her icy stare. "I thought, uh, maybe after graduation we could, y'know, go somewhere." He glanced over his shoulder. Not at her, but in her general direction. "Together."

Tammy smiled. It was not a good smile. Then again, her good smiles weren't really very good either if someone knew the dark thoughts behind them.

"A road trip?" she asked.

"Uh . . . yeah."

"After graduation."

"Uh . . . yeah."

"Together."

He bit the inside of his cheek and tapped his pencil against the desk. "I was thinking we could maybe go to Vegas. I've always wanted to go to Vegas."

She smiled wider. "Sounds like fun."

"Yeah. We could go to the strip. Maybe see one of those big shows. I mean, I know we won't have much money by then, but we can still have a good time."

Her face fell blank. The pencil in Chad's hand snapped in two.

"Man, you are such a dumbass," she muttered.

"But I thought . . ."

"You didn't think, Chad. You never think."

He slammed his fist into his palm. "Goddamn it, Tammy. Stop callin' me stupid. You're always callin' me stupid."

"That's because you are stupid."

"You're such a bitch." He crumpled up his copied home-work, stuffed it in his pocket, and headed toward the door.

It slammed shut all by itself.

"Sit down, Chad."

"Fuck you."

He reached for the knob and got a jolt that numbed his forearm and stopped him cold.

"I said, sit down."

Chad obeyed. He massaged the gooey muscles of his wrist.

Her father shouted from the living room.

She pointed to the door, and it opened wide enough to suit parental regulations. "Sorry, Dad!"

Chad blew on his deadened fingertips in an effort to revive some feeling.

"Stop being such a wuss," she grumbled.

He hunched over, holding his numb hand to his chest. He stared at the floor, unable to look her in the eye. Chad didn't really understand any of the black magic they dabbled in. She just told him what to do, and he did it. It'd started with naked chanting which he had thoroughly enjoyed, even if it did in-volve memorizing long strings of tongue-twisting syllables. And it just kept getting weirder and weirder. None of which bothered him too much as long as he and Tammy got to spend time together. Although the sex had a lot to do with it, it wasn't the only reason. He liked her. Or, at least, he had at one time.

He still did, he had to admit to himself. Even if she did scare the crap out of him more and more every day as the darkness in her soul grew with her unnatural powers. She had a knack for burying that darkness beneath a schoolgirl's fa-cade, but either it was beginning to overwhelm her or he was just better at spotting it. Either way, he didn't know how much longer he could pretend he didn't see it.

And there was that whole end-of-the-world dilemma to add to his problems. He wasn't a big fan of the world, and the part about becoming living gods sounded cool enough. But he had doubts.

"What if it doesn't work?"

"It will."

"But you said that this ritual thing we're gonna do will bring these badass demons to Earth."

"Old gods," she corrected. "Not demons."

"Whatever. So these old gods come to Earth, and they're gonna be so grateful that they'll give us all this power 'cuz we freed them."

"That's right." She grinned a thin, patronizing sneer.

"But you said that they'll also destroy the world."

She rubbed her eyes with her palms. She was tired of explaining it to him. "They shall remake it, undo the corruption of man, and forge it in their image."

Chad struggled to find a distinction. "No more Vegas?"

"No more Vegas."

"And these old god guys, they're, like, evil, right?"

"Good and evil are mortal constraints. The old gods are beyond morality."

"Uh . . . right. So, I guess what I'm trying to ask is, if these god dudes are so powerful and so unconstrained, then how do we know they'll carry out their end of the deal?"

"They will."

"But how do you know for sure?"

Her voice dropped to a rough whisper.

"Because I know."

Chad hardly felt reassured.

Tammy could sense his doubt. She had little patience for unbelievers. Her abridged *Necronomicon* had a brief chapter on cult maintenance. It laid out a simple and effective method of dealing with skeptical followers.

> *It is inevitable that any cult will eventually find itself*
> *beset by the occasional disciple of questionable faith. These lost*
> *children should be herded gently back into unswerving loyalty.*
> *If this does not work, experience tells us that while a loyal*
> *follower is preferred over a dead follower, a dead follower is*
> *preferred over a skeptic. One bad apple spoils the bunch. Using*
> *a lost soul in a ritual sacrifice, particularly one involving the*
> *rest of the cult, can not only squeeze one last drop of usefulness*
> *out of a discarded member, but can also serve to bring about*
> *a unity to your happy family and dissuade any more skeptics*
> *from emerging.*

It was good advice, but she couldn't afford to sacrifice Chad. Not yet. He was her only follower. And, though she was slow to admit it, she'd actually grown a little fond of him. He was handy to have around at times, and she was saving his death for a special occasion.

She was left with only one other alternative. She swallowed her revulsion and put forth the soft smile she saved for these moments.

"Baby, come here."

She patted the spot beside her on the bed. He hesitated. She crossed and uncrossed her legs to help him along. When that didn't work, she ran her fingers along the inside of her thigh. That did the trick. He sat beside her, and she took his jolted hand.

"I'm sorry, baby. Did I hurt you?"

"It's okay."

"I shouldn't have done that." She gently kissed his fingertips, one by one. "Do you forgive me?"

He stuck out his lower lip and kicked his heel against the bed. "I don't know. Maybe." He still refused to look at her.

She leaned close to his ear and called upon the sultry voice she'd honed through hours of practice. "C'mon, Chad. Don't be mad."

His head slowly turned toward her until their faces were inches apart. She pulled back just a little. "Let me worry about the details. That's my job."

She could almost hear every drop of saliva evaporate in his mouth. "But what's my job?" he asked dryly.

"Your job is to keep me happy."

He swallowed a deep gulp of air and opened his mouth to say something else. Tammy put a finger to his parted lips.

"Can you do that, Chad? Can you keep me happy? Because if I'm happy, then you'll be happy." She suppressed a gag. "Very, very happy."

If she could kiss him, he would be hers again. But her father had strict rules about things that were allowed in her bedroom. Making out was not on that list, and she didn't take needless chances.

Chad's hormonally deluged mind struggled to form a single, cohesive thought. Tammy gave him the time he needed to extract one. Finally, he made eye contact, and from there, his gaze rolled down to her lips, then chest, then all the other good parts along the way to her toes.

"Okay, but I don't like it when you call me stupid."

"Of course. I shouldn't have done that. I won't do it again."

Chad grinned stupidly, confirming he was hers again.

Her bedroom door opened, and her father poked his head in the room just long enough to tell her it was half past nine. No boys after nine-thirty. It was another of her dad's dumb rules. She could hang out with Chad late at night, just as long as it wasn't in her bedroom. Never mind that it was the one place in the world they'd never do any of the things her dad objected to, and never mind that out of the house, she and Chad had screwed around plenty of times. Parental rules had little to do with logic. They were just regulations they'd had to suffer through when they were kids and now had to inflict on their own offspring. Existence was merely an endless rotation. A led to B led to C all the way to Z which looped back to A. The world was a bad TV show stuck in reruns and in desperate need of cancellation. Which was why she was so looking forward to ending it.

Chad gathered up his books and homework, and she walked him to his motorcycle.

"Hey, how come you never use any of your magic stuff on your parents?" he asked as he climbed on the bike.

She almost called him stupid again but bit her lip.

"Because that magic stuff isn't as easy as I make it look."

"Yeah, but I bet you could do that mind-control thing on them real easy. Just to get them off your back." He wiggled his fingers at her and made a serious face.

His ignorance was almost cute in a ridiculous sort of way. For one moment, she forgot how much he annoyed her.

He started the engine. "So you wanna do sumthin' tomorrow?"

In Chad's lexicon, "Sumthin'" translated into hanging around somewhere for an hour or so before finding a place to screw. He was due for a maintenance jump anyway.

"How about tonight?"

"What about your dad?"

"He won't care." She chuckled. "Just as long as we're not in my room." She hopped on the bike behind him, wrapping her arms low around his waist, resting her chin on his shoulder and breathing on his ear.

"Can't we put off the apocalypse until after graduation?"

"Chad."

"Alright, alright." He revved the engine. "I was just askin'."

TWENTY-TWO

Rockwood General Supply was a combination grocery, feed store, and used-car lot. Like much of the architecture of the town, the building was without any attempts at decoration. Its name was painted on each of the white walls in stenciled black letters. The used-car inventory consisted of three battered pickup trucks in various states of disrepair and a Volvo on cinderblocks that nonetheless "ran like a dream" according to a cardboard sign under the windshield wipers. Broken-down cars aside, the store was well stocked. Duke was able to find most of the things on Earl's list. Not that there was much hard-to-find stuff on it. Most of it was pretty basic.

There was magic in the mundane. Hector had once told him that a practitioner with three yards of duct tape, a PEZ dispenser, a CD player, and a pair of oversized clown shoes was responsible for the fall of the Roman Empire. Duke never really understood how that worked, considering the Roman Empire had already fallen long before any of those items were available. But magic was never bothered by paradoxes like that. Supposedly, the average bathroom had all the necessary bits and pieces to resurrect the dead or exorcise an evil spirit. Of course, one needed an impressive level of talent to pull off something like that. Which was why most practitioners made it easier on themselves by throwing in weird doodles painted in blood, waving around exotic props, and chanting in an excessively dramatic fashion. The way Hector had put it, the forces invisible generally like a good show.

Duke prowled the aisles twice. He was still missing a couple of items when he went to the register.

"Evening, son," the short old woman replied. "Find everything alright?"

He checked his list. "I need candles."

"We got some back thataway."

"They're white. I need blue."

"Don't think we got any of those." She turned toward the back of the building and shouted. "Hey, Bill! Bill! Goddamn it, Bill, you lazy son of a bitch!"

The door in the back marked "Employees Only" opened a crack. Nobody came out, but a voice emerged.

"Yeah? What?"

"We got any candles?"

"Aisle six!"

"Those are white! This feller wants blue!"

"Blue? What for?"

The register lady shook her head. "Ain't none of our business! Just go check if we got any!"

"We don't got any!" Bill's voice yelled back immediately.

"Did'ja check?"

"I said, we ain't got any, Mary!"

"Did'ja check?"

"Hell's bells, Mary! I know what we got back here!"

"Just check already, you worthless . . ."

"Alright, alright! I'm checking!"

"You better really check!" Mary growled. "I'll know if you don't!"

The door slammed shut.

Mary began ringing Duke up. "Sorry 'bout that, son."

"S'alright."

The cash register was an antique. It clanged and clicked with each push of the keys.

"Hey, Duke!"

Tammy bounced through the store's front doors, followed by a woman he guessed to be her mother. She skipped by his side.

"Hey," he mumbled back.

"What'cha doin'?"

"Shopping."

"Cool."

Bill's door opened. "Ain't got no blue candles back here!"

"You sure?" Mary asked.

"Yeah!"

She shrugged at Duke. "Sorry, son."

"That's okay. No big deal." He ran his finger down to the next item on his list. They probably wouldn't have it, but in a town like Rockwood there was no way of knowing unless you asked.

"Got any powdered raven's eye?"

"Might. Let me check. Hey, Bill! Bill, you no-good bastard!"

The door opened a crack again, and Bill and Mary spent a minute shouting at one another before he agreed to go and check. While they did, Duke went down the aisles to retrieve some white candles and a can of blue spray paint. Tammy tagged along.

"So what'cha gonna do with all that stuff," she asked.

"Cast a magic spell."

"Really? Like a love spell or something?"

"Don't know."

Tammy's mother called her away, much to Duke's relief. He'd always made fun of Earl for complaining about the attentions of nubile young girls. Now he finally understood Earl's dilemma. The human portion of Duke's soul didn't want to take unnecessary advantage of Tammy. The raging beast simmering just below the surface had no such constraints. It saw Tammy as a potential and all-too-willing mate. The beast threw pornographic flashes across his consciousness. He pushed them back.

"Is this enough, son?"

"Huh?"

Mary shook a plastic bag with a few ounces of dried raven's eye. "Is this enough? It's all we got."

"Uh. Yeah. That'll do."

"Anything else?"

"Got any belladonna?"

Bill, who now stood beside Mary, was a short, stocky man who looked as if his skin had been left to tan in the desert sun for the last four hundred years. "Don't think we got any."

Mary jabbed an elbow in his ribs. "Why don't you go check?"

" 'Cuz I'm pretty sure we don't got any."

"Well, why don't you make sure?"

He shot her a hard glare. She shot back a harder glare. Bill withered and shuffled into the back room, mumbling.

While Duke and Mary waited for his return, Tammy and her mother went about their shopping. Duke tried not to watch Tammy as she bent to retrieve Liquid-Plumr or stretched on her tiptoes to reach the canned goods on the really high shelves. He couldn't help himself. The beast grew stronger as the moon grew fuller. By the month's end, he doubted he could resist her. Hopefully, she'd be bored with him by then. Or his business with the diner would be done, and he'd leave Rockwood and temptation behind.

If not . . .

Well, if not, then it was only a matter of time.

Tammy caught him staring at her. She smiled in a way that was both full of girlish innocence and seductive allure. Mary caught him staring, too, and shook her head in a most disapproving fashion. Bill was too busy staring himself to catch anyone else.

He tore his eyes from Tammy's jeans just long enough to toss a paper bag on the counter. "Belladonna. Anything else you wantin' there, son?"

"No. That's it."

Duke paid the bill, dipping deep into his nearly empty pockets. Freeing Earl's girlfriend was draining their limited resources. Duke hoped she was worth it. Cathy was bound to find out what an asshole Earl was. If she could see the positive traits buried beneath his avalanche of character flaws, then they might stand a chance. If she didn't, and Duke didn't reckon she would, she'd take off. Earl would take it hard. The poor bastard had it bad for the girl. If things went south, he'd be a real son of a bitch for the next couple of months. Duke wasn't looking forward to it.

In the parking lot, Marshall Kopp's cruiser pulled up. The sheriff rolled down his window and stuck out his head. "Mornin', Duke."

"Sheriff."

"How are things at the diner?"

"Gettin' worse."

"I was afraid of that. I been pretty busy myself, lately. Rained horny toads over at the trailer park, and I found Curtis Mayfair running 'round last night, covered in green sludge, rambling about alien abductions. And the shrieking yucca at Lover's Grove has stopped screaming and started laughing. That ain't never a good sign. Sumthin's brewing. Sumthin' bad." The sheriff ducked his head in the cruiser just long enough to take a drink of soda.

"I've been checking all the cult hot spots: Sander's Mill, the old Robertson place, Canin Field. Every place that's lonely and deserted that a bunch might be able to get together and practice black magic."

"Any luck?"

"None so far. My guess is they know we're lookin' for 'em and are keepin' a low profile. But it's only a matter of time before they slip up. And you know what they say, it's always the last place you look."

"Yup." Duke tossed his sack of magical supplies in his pickup's cab. He climbed in after it.

"See ya' 'round, Duke."

The cruiser took off.

Duke started the truck. He glanced back at the store. Tammy waved from the doors and blew him a kiss. He caught her scent lingering in the breeze. She smelled good. Young, eager, and fertile. A perfect mate. Every muscle in his body tightened. The steering wheel bent in his grip. The impression of his large hands was left in the imitation leather.

"Goddamn."

Drawing on his dwindling reserves of self-control, he fled from Rockwood General Supply and Auto Sales at a leisurely forty miles per hour.

TWENTY-THREE

Reality is like a fruitcake; Pretty enough to look at but with all sorts of nasty things lurking just beneath the surface. Ancient things, older than time itself, smothered beneath the crushing interdimensional weight of what mortals, in their limited understanding, would call existence. These are the dark things: forgotten shadows of what once was but no longer is, malign dreams of what might have been yet should never be, and twisted phantoms of entities that never truly lived but nonetheless cannot die. Most horrible of these nightmares, if such a value could truly be measured, are the old gods. Locked away in the deepest, darkest pit like the hideous, redheaded stepchild of Creation shoved to the back of the cosmic closet to be ignored.

Some things refuse to be ignored.

To mix metaphors, the closet door in Gil's All Night Diner opened just a crack, and a nasty walnut slipped through. A nasty, rotten walnut eager to chip the tooth of all that was good and decent.

At the moment, Loretta was blissfully unaware of this fact. Just as she was unaware of the spectral terrier sitting in the corner of the kitchen, watching her clean the grill.

Napoleon did not fully understand his current state of existence. He only knew that most people could not see him anymore. He vaguely remembered chasing a jackrabbit across a street and getting squashed by a pickup. He remembered floating over the flattened body of a dog that looked very much like him, but obviously couldn't be. Then there was the light. It called to him in a chorus of playful barks and howls. The glorious scent of raw hamburger and sausage drew him closer. His canine mind knew that on the other side of that light was a paradise of unending mountains of liver-flavored treats and things in constant need of being peed on and slow rabbits. Though not too slow. He drifted into the light, but something made him stop. The jackrabbit that had led him to his untimely demise sat by the road. A rabbit was a rabbit, and Napoleon decided that this one was not getting away so easily. He descended to earth, and the light disappeared. He didn't notice.

He caught his quarry though he quickly discovered there wasn't much his immaterial body could do to it. Still, it had been a good chase, and that was enough.

Loretta scraped at a stubborn greasy blob with a spatula. Grunting, she shifted her immense weight from one side to another. Her ample butt shook as she chipped away at her chore, one stubborn, brown fleck at a time.

Napoleon studied the trembling rear end. Cheeks tightened and unclenched rhythmically, much like a pair of sumo wrestlers struggling beneath a cotton tarp. The dance stopped just long enough for Loretta to wipe the sweat from her face and take a long drink from the soda beside her. Then it was back to work.

Napoleon could have watched her for hours. Since dying, he'd become something of a people watcher. They were fascinating creatures, and he had yet to understand much of anything they did, except for eating, mating, and relieving themselves. And even the way they did that last thing was odd. But not understanding humans made them all the more interesting. Of course, there were other interesting things besides people. Slimy, green tentacles slithering from beneath refrigerators for example.

The dog jumped to alert and bounded between the thing under the refrigerator and Loretta. He growled as the tentacles slipped forward. When that didn't work, he barked furiously in an effort to show he meant business and to alert her to the danger reaching for her ankles.

She just ignored him.

Finally, he snapped at the end of a tentacle. He didn't expect to actually bite it and was pleasantly surprised when his teeth connected.

Dogs, even ghostly ones, understood very little of the true workings of the universe. Less than even human beings, if such a thing can be possible. Napoleon didn't know that the thing under the refrigerator existed in a cross-dimensional state, simultaneously dwelling across two dozen or so planes of existence. And that one of those planes happened to be the ectoplasmic sphere, thus allowing ghosts to interact with the thing. He only knew that he could bite this, and so he bit harder. He sank his teeth in the squishy flesh. It tasted horrible, but it'd been a long time since he'd tasted anything, so he relished it.

The thing under the refrigerator squealed.

Loretta turned to see a mass of tentacles whipping about in a twisting dance. It lashed violently from side to side. Napoleon's jaws slipped loose, and he was sent flying into a wall with enough force to crack the spine of a material terrier. Napoleon just kept going, passing out of the kitchen.

The thing under the refrigerator rumbled. The rusty Frigidaire rocked to one side, nearly tipping over. Tentacles grayed and shimmered as if they might fade away. They probed the floor and felt along the counters. A limb snatched up a blender and tossed it away. It shattered against the floor.

Something about the thing under the refrigerator scared Loretta, and she had never been easily scared. Regular battles with the walking dead had only made her more stubborn. The thing was unpleasant to look at, a slithering, slimy mass of unnatural horror, but she'd seen worse. It wasn't the form of the thing that bothered her. It was the almost psychic realization that this thing, whatever the hell it was, was completely alien. As far beyond mortal comprehension as anything could be.

And just as she knew this without knowing, she knew that this was just a tiny piece of the thing. Its whole body would smother the Earth, and there was nothing the thing under the refrigerator wanted more than this.

"Not in my kitchen, you heathen demon."

Pushing away her terror, she grabbed a hanging cleaver and hacked at one of the writhing tendrils. The blade sliced through greenish, boneless flesh. The thing screeched. The bit of severed tentacle fell to the floor and burst into flame even as a new tip grew for its damaged limb.

"Damnation."

Something moved beneath the floor. The tile rose and fell in liquid waves. The cabinets opened all at once. More tentacles poked their way through the back of the cupboards that, by Loretta's reckoning, had become blackened portals to Hell. This was entirely wrong. Hell was a Candy Land compared to the dark void the thing hailed from. Eyes and tongues and bleeding orifices covered the tentacles in no particular pattern other than chaos. Boils grew and popped, dripping a thick, yellow syrup.

Loretta made her way to the kitchen door, mere feet away. She ducked and wove between the misshapen limbs. One got too close for comfort until she backed it off with a strike of her cleaver. She didn't know what to expect on the other side of the door. She half-expected a giant eye or swirling vortex of nothingness.

Instead, she found Duke. Napoleon stood by his side, though she didn't see the ghost.

"What's wrong?" he asked.

"It's in the kitchen."

"What's in the kitchen?"

She struggled to put it in words. There was only one description that came to mind. "Some thing."

Napoleon hopped in front of the door, unleashing a hail of vicious barks. At least as vicious as a terrier was able to bark.

Duke guided her aside with a gentle hand and pushed open the door.

There was nothing there. Nothing but the kitchen, some open cupboards, a broken blender, and a slightly askew refrigerator.

"It was here. Under there. In there. And there. In the floor. Everywhere."

Duke and Loretta searched the room top to bottom. There wasn't a single tentacle or hell portal to be found.

"I saw it," she said.

"I believe you, but whatever it was, it's not here now."

"But where could it have gotten to?"

Duke shrugged. He had no answers.

The storeroom door opened slowly, and Earl emerged, sleepy-eyed and sluggish. It was the middle of the day. He should have been sleeping. It took a hell of a lot to get the undead up before dusk.

"We are in some serious shit, Duke."

Earl collapsed, sprawling across a counter. Duke checked him, but he was asleep again.

"Is he okay?" Loretta asked.

Duke tossed the thin vampire over his shoulder and returned him to his trunk.

"What did he mean?"

"We'll have to wait till he wakes up again to ask," Duke replied. "But I can tell you one thing. It ain't gonna be good news."

Meanwhile, back in the kitchen, Napoleon spotted a lingering tentacle behind the refrigerator. The swollen, purple eye on its tip and the dog engaged in a short staring contest. Napoleon snarled. The thing behind the refrigerator vanished into a shadow and back into the cosmic basement.

With a virile yip, the terrier trotted back to Duke's side.

TWENTY-FOUR

When dusk rolled around, Earl climbed out of his trunk and poured himself a cup of coffee that he downed in two-point-four seconds.

"It's evil."

He poured another, which he gulped down in two-point-one.

"Kinda figured that already, Earl," Duke said.

Earl watched the swirling coffee in the pot. "You don't get it, Duke. I'm not talking about plain ol', nasty sort of evil. I'm talking 'bout evil with a capital 'E'. Something so foul and sinister that there aren't even words to really describe it."

"Really, really evil," Duke suggested.

Earl slammed his empty coffee mug against the counter. It cracked in two. "Damn it, you stupid son of a bitch! You aren't listenin' to me." He grabbed a new, unbroken mug and the coffeepot and sat at the table with Duke and Loretta. "She, at least, saw it. She knows what I'm talkin' about."

Loretta nodded. "He's right."

"Really, really pissed off, badass, evil," Duke said. "I got it."

"No, you don't." Earl sighed. "You know how it works with me, Duke. When I'm sleepin', my mind shuts off with my body, but some part of it is still working." He turned to Loretta. "Sort'a like a supernatural radio. Now most things, even really bad things, don't have enough power to register. When something does, it's always pretty Goddamn serious."

"Like what?" she asked.

"Well, there was that earthquake in Mexico while back. Radiated enough psychic suffering that I woke up for about ten seconds or so. And then there was that time when the Nazis invaded Poland. I just knew that was going to be trouble." He did his coffee routine again. "And when they canceled *The Green Hornet*, I couldn't get back to sleep for half-an-hour. Man, I loved that show."

"Kato kicked ass," Duke agreed.

"Anyway, all that stuff is nuthin' compared to the vibe I picked up this afternoon when that thing appeared in the kitchen. If you put all that together with every psychic blip I've ever detected in my sleep of death, you still wouldn't equal the dark evil that thing shoved in my head." He shuddered at the recollection. "Lucky for me, my mind blocked out most of it. Otherwise, I'd be too crazy to talk right now. Maybe ever again."

Duke nodded.

Earl snorted. "Look, you dipshit. Most people think to be really evil you have to have a choice. That you can't be really bad unless you can be good. They're wrong. Real evil, true evil, not just that kill-everybody-you-don't-like or nuke-a-country-'cuz-you-don't-care-for-the-way-they-spell-its-name kind of evil, comes from not having any good in you. *Ever.*

"People aren't made like that. Everybody's got some good in 'em. Or had some at some point. But this thing, it never has. It's absolute and eternal . . ." He rubbed his temples, looking in vain for the right word.

"I got it, Earl. It's evil. More evil than I can ever understand. So stop tryin' to get me to understand already."

Earl emptied the last of the pot in his mug. "The point I'm really tryin' to make is that it's not alone. There's a lot more right behind it, just like it. Some even worse, I think."

"Worse than absolute evil."

"I told you, you can't understand."

Duke cracked his knuckles. "Whatever you say."

"What I'm gettin' to, Duke, if you'd stop interrupting me, is that I'm not stickin' around this place anymore. I'm taking off. With or without you."

Duke drew in a deep breath. His broad chest inflated. His shirt collar popped a stitch. He fixed Earl with his typical stone-faced lack of expression. His eyes narrowed the tiniest fraction. His brow furrowed in barely noticeable lines.

"You runnin' away then?"

Earl turned away under the guise of returning the coffeepot to its place, but was really hiding his inability to look Duke in the eye.

"Yeah."

Duke rose from his chair very, very slowly.

Earl swallowed a nervous twitch. The average vampire wasn't much of a match for the average werewolf in a knock-down-drag-out fight. The undead were mostly shadow and stealth, phantoms of flesh designed to prowl the night. Werewolves were built to kill, plain and simple. Earl had seen Duke slaughter five vampire punks in Little Rock. They'd gotten in a few good shots, but when it was all over, they'd tasted final death while Duke had only lost an arm.

Each of those punks individually had been tougher than Earl. A lot tougher.

He didn't think Duke would really kill him. Duke was particular about who he killed. But he could still kick the unliving shit out of Earl without much effort.

Keys clattered on the counter beside him.

"Take the truck."

"Did you get my stuff?" Earl asked Duke.

"In the storeroom. By your trunk."

"Thanks." He stuffed the keys in his pocket. "Sorry, Loretta."

She smiled softly. "That's alright. I understand. Hell, if I had a brain, I'd be leaving myself."

Napoleon, who up to now had been occupied with the death throes of a cockroach, perked up his ears and turned to the walk-in freezer door. He loudly sniffed the metal door from one end to another and back again. Then he started growling.

Duke and Earl watched the door suspiciously, but it didn't do anything. Napoleon's growling graduated to angry, staccato barking. Loretta couldn't see or hear him, but she could see the nervousness on Earl's face.

"What? Did'ja hear somethin'?"

Napoleon bent on his front legs. His tail fell flat. Cautiously, he stuck his head and half his immaterial body through the door. He barked once, quickly withdrew, and ran behind Duke with a whimper.

Duke took a step forward, reaching for the handle.

"Don't open it," Earl said.

"Got to."

"No, you don't. Just let whatever is in there be."

"What?" Loretta asked. "What's in there?"

"Something evil, I bet."

"Only one way to find out." Duke lifted the handle, and soft, white frost slipped through the cracked door.

Earl threw his thin frame against it, slamming it shut. "Damn it, Duke. Why do we have to find out at all? Who says we want to find out? I don't want to. How 'bout you, Loretta?"

"Just give me a sec." She retrieved her shotgun and aimed at the door. "Alright, I'm ready."

Earl threw up his arms. "Aw, shit. Fine. Open the Goddamn thing. But don't say I didn't warn you when some horrible, otherdimensional, squidoid fucking thing rips you a new asshole."

He stepped aside, shaking his head.

"Nobody ever listens to me."

"On three," Duke said.

Loretta cocked the hammers of her shotgun.

Napoleon offered up halfhearted barks even as he backed away.

"One."

"Can't leave well enough alone," Earl mumbled. "Can't leave the unholy hellbeast in the freezer."

"Two."

"Oh no. God forbid. Much better to get our eyes eaten and our souls ripped out."

"Three."

Duke threw wide the door. The unnaturally thick mist spilled across the kitchen floor in an ankle-deep fog. The thing in the freezer took one clumsy step forward. The humanoid shape was nothing more than slimy skin draped over bones. Its eyes thrust forth from their sockets on long stalks that swept the room.

Loretta lowered her shotgun a few inches. "Gil?"

Gil Wilson's thin form opened its mouth as if to speak. A yellow paste dripped from its lips.

"Shoot it!" Earl shouted.

"But, it's Gil. I can't just . . ."

Gil groaned, extending his arms toward Duke. The werewolf backed away. If Earl didn't know better, he'd have thought Duke was afraid. But nothing scared Duke.

"It's not Gil! It's just something in Gil's body!"

"But . . ."

Gil literally twisted in Earl's direction. The body shifted and turned in ways that would have been impossible with joints and bones in the way. Its skin swelled, as if there were other entities lurking just below the surface, waiting to break free.

"Shoot the fuckin' thing!"

She fired both barrels into it. The body disintegrated. Most of it just disappeared like a popped bubble. The limbs and head fell to the floor. The fog rolled into the freezer, sucked into an invisible hole in the back. The bits and pieces started melting amidst agonized squeals.

Duke, Earl, and Loretta warily gathered together at the door, watching what was left of Gil drip away into nonexistence.

"What the hell happened to him?" she asked.

Duke knelt down, though he didn't touch the pieces. "You sure that was Gil Wilson, Loretta?"

She nodded. "Pretty sure. Kind'a hard to tell." The arms and legs were gone, but the fleshless skull remained. She prodded it with her shotgun. "This doesn't make any sense. I mean, I've been in and out of this freezer hundreds of times. He couldn't have been in there all that time. There's no place to hide. So where in the Lord's name has he been?"

"Hell," Earl answered. "He's been in hell. 'Least, his body has. And something tried to ride it back out again."

The eyes popped from the sockets again. Eight spider-like legs thrust from underneath the skull. The skull sprang up and over their heads, hit the tile, and scrambled toward the kitchen door.

Napoleon stopped its flight. The ghost dog snapped and snarled, holding the skull at bay. They circled warily. The skull squirted a dark, red liquid from its nose. Napoleon whined.

Duke brought down one immense sneaker on the abominable headbone. It shattered into a gooey mess. The skull let loose with one last ear-shattering shriek.

Earl checked Napoleon. A chunk of the dog's shoulder was gone, bubbling and hissing. Ectoplasm was not flesh. It was a construction to house the bodiless soul. The stuff of spirits was mostly indestructible, but there were ways to kill a ghost. Real, physical ways if one had the means.

Napoleon lay on the floor as more and more of his body dissolved.

"Shit!" Earl carefully picked up the dog and cradled it in his arms. "Come on, little guy. Don't die on me now."

The acid had eaten away a leg. It kept consuming, but it was slowing. Earl prayed it would stop. He didn't want to tell Cathy her dead dog was really dead.

Napoleon raised his head with pained eyes he could barely keep open. With one final whimper, his head dissolved. But the acid finally stopped eating away.

"Yes."

He clutched the headless, three-legged specter to his chest. Napoleon just needed time to recover now. Hopefully, he'd get back his missing parts, but even if he didn't, a ghost didn't technically need them. It'd take some getting used to, but, at least, he'd live. Sort of.

Loretta saw only Earl cradling empty air. "Is he alright?" she asked Duke.

Duke nodded. He didn't bother explaining.

Earl put Napoleon in his trunk to rest. Then he grabbed his stuff and headed out the door, stopping just long enough to glance down at the slimy remains of brains and bones.

"Go get her, Earl," Duke sighed, scraping the sludge from the soles of his sneaker with a spatula. "Sooner you free your girlfriend, sooner you can get goin'."

Earl didn't know why he should feel bad about leaving. Duke was a grown man. If he didn't have enough sense to get away from Gil's All Night Diner while he still could, it wasn't Earl's fault. But he felt bad anyway. Duke had always been there for him. He'd slept a little easier every day knowing Duke was watching his back. And now, at the first sign of trouble, he was taking off.

"Duke . . ." He struggled with the words. "I just want you to know that I, uh, well . . ."

Duke stopped cleaning gunk off his shoes. They stared at each other amid the quiet splashing of Loretta mopping up extradimensional brain spider goo.

"Damn it, why do you gotta go and make this so fuckin' hard?"

Earl switched his sack from one hand to the other and back again.

"I'm sorry. That's all I wanted to say."

Duke's face remained as blank as ever.

Earl turned to the doors. "You asshole."

"See you around, Earl."

Halfway out the kitchen, the vampire turned. Duke was back to salvaging his sneakers.

"See you around, Duke."

TWENTY-FIVE

Most of Earl's self-loathing disappeared the moment he saw Cathy. She smiled, and he almost forgot about deserting Duke.

"Hey, where's Napoleon?"

"He's in the diner. Playing with Duke." He felt bad about lying to her, but he didn't want her to worry needlessly. He held up the paper bag. "I think I'm ready to cast the spell tonight."

"Already?"

"Well, I can't actually cast it until around eight-thirty. But I can set it up."

"Why eight-thirty?"

"'Cuz that's when the metaphysical atmosphere is most receptive to spectral unchaining."

"Wow. I thought you didn't know much about magic."

He shrugged. "I get by."

Truthfully, his experience was rather limited. The "metaphysical atmosphere" was Hector's wording. Not his. But he was willing to fake a greater understanding if it impressed her.

"So how's this work?"

He removed items from the bag, explaining their purpose. "The blue candles represent wind and water, elemental forces that are ever free. And I'll use this bag of salt to form the circle of ectoplasmic binding. And I'll paint the runes 'round the circle with this." He shook the can of spray paint. "It's red 'cuz that's the color of earth, the force that anchors you."

He grinned, swelling with pride.

"Runes. Like the runes Odin gave up his eye for?"

Rather than admit he didn't know who the hell that was, he simply nodded.

"Tell me more." She pointed to the items he'd yet to get to. "What's all that for?"

Earl's grin faded away. He couldn't remember anything Hector had said about the rest of it. He flipped through his notes. They only told him how to use them. He'd neglected to write down all of Hector's arcane terminology.

Bravely, he pressed on.

"Well, this, uh, dried raven's eye is used to call the, uh, nature spirits. Specifically the great bird fathers so that they might, uh, chase away the grave fiends."

"Grave fiends?"

"Yeah." He coughed to cover an awkward pause while he gathered his thoughts. "They're these nasty things that, uh, might screw things up if we're not careful. Sort'a like gremlins that haunt graveyards."

"I've never seen any."

"You wouldn't. They're invisible."

"So am I."

"Yeah, but they're invisible in a different way. They're all around. Trust me."

"If you say so."

He snatched up something else to distract her. "This belladonna is called the enchanter's herb. It just makes magic easier when you burn it."

"Really? Why?"

"It's kind'a complicated." He checked his watch. "I better get this set up. No point waiting until the last minute."

He started with the runes Hector had described over the phone. He hoped they were done right. Arcane symbols weren't standardized like the alphabet. No one really understood how they worked. They only knew that if you drew a triangle in a circle in a square in just the right way, you could get something unnatural to happen.

After he finished the last rune around Cathy's grave, they all shimmered with soft red light.

"That means they're ready," he explained.

The glow faded, but the runes started moving. Not in an obvious way—it was more like he could sense them stirring, shifting when not being watched. And when he turned back to look at them again, they did indeed look different. Or maybe not.

Next he placed the blue candles between the runes to surround the grave. He lit each and mumbled a quick incantation scribbled on his notepad. When the flame burned bright red, he poured the circle of salt and muttered a second, longer incantation. He knew he'd done it right when the wind didn't blow the salt away. The setup was complete. The circle could only be broken by an act of will.

He stood back and studied his work. A magic circle worthy of Merlin himself. Or maybe Merlin's amateur, penniless half-brother. But looks weren't important as long as it did the trick.

They still had forty-five minutes before the casting. Cathy and Earl killed the time by lying on their backs and staring at the stars.

She pointed. "That one right there is my favorite. I don't know why. It's not the brightest or the biggest, but there's just something about it."

"It's nice," Earl agreed.

"Sometimes I make up my own constellations. Like over there, that's the Goose. And just below that is the Happy Face. And over there is the Big Dipper."

"There's already a Big Dipper."

"I didn't say I was very good at it."

They chuckled, sliding closer. She turned on her side and laid a hand on his chest. He stroked her hair. The ectoplasmic strands slipped through his fingers, light as gossamer. He suddenly realized how mortal he was.

Vampires liked to think of themselves as eternal. But, in the end, their lives were measured in moments. Just like the living. Certainly there were a lot more moments, but quantity was highly overrated. He would have traded the last ninety-plus years of his life to make this particular moment last just a little longer. But time waited for no one, mortal or immortal. He tried not to think about it, to just enjoy it while it lasted.

"Earl?"

"Yeah?"

"Can vampires bite ghosts?"

"Sure. I've never done it myself, but I hear it's a lot like suckin' down Jell-O."

"What else can vampires and ghosts do?"

"Well, ectoplasm is pretty much the same as flesh and blood for the undead."

"How much like it?"

"Just like it. In all the important ways."

"All the important ways?"

"Yeah, sure. Why?"

She took his hand and guided it to her waist.

He was caught completely by surprise. She was so pretty and so wonderful, he couldn't imagine her wasting her time with him. But she didn't have much choice really. The romantic opportunities of a graveyard guardian were limited, at best.

She glided over him. He lost his train of thought in her smoldering eyes. She kissed him. He instinctively fumbled for her bra only to discover she wasn't wearing one. Or any clothes at all, for that matter. His hands ran down her back. Her ectoplasmic skin was so smooth and soft. He couldn't imagine anything more perfect than the spot on the small of her back where his fingers came to rest.

She undid his overalls.

He imagined what he might look like to the casual observer. A naked man writhing and rolling in the dirt with his phantom lover. Her hair brushed his neck as she kissed his chest, and he found he didn't care.

A cynical little voice whispered, "It's not you. She'd like anyone after all these years alone." But it was a very small voice, easy enough to push away in the moment.

Another moment that lasted not nearly long enough.

Naked, Earl lay in the dirt and watched Cathy breathe.

Ghosts weren't supposed to breathe, but she did anyway. She snuggled closer, and he could feel the faint beat of her heart. It was only an incredible simulation, but he marveled at how much humanity she still had after all these years of being dead. While he'd done his best to avoid specters, he'd met more than enough to realize how rare that was.

She caught him staring. "What?"

"Nuthin'."

"What are you thinking?"

"Nuthin'."

Smiling, she kissed him. "That was nice. Thank you."

He shifted, trying to work some pointed pebbles under his spine to a less bothersome position without actually getting up.

"Just nice?"

Another bad thing about being a vampire was the expectations created by an irresponsible media. When it came to making love, there were higher standards for the undead. Standards he fell well short of.

"Very nice," she replied. "You were great."

He blushed for the first time in two decades.

"Of course, it has been a while," Cathy added. "I'm pretty damn easy."

They laughed.

"What time is it?"

Earl checked his watch. "Eight-fifteen."

"We better get ready then."

"Yeah. We better."

Neither moved. Minutes passed in contented silence.

Finally, with five minutes until casting, Cathy slid away from him. She stood. Spectral clothing materialized on her body again. Earl had to get dressed the old-fashioned way.

"So am I supposed to stand in the circle?" she asked.

"You don't got to do anything, actually. Your grave is the source of the binding. I'm really doing the magic on that."

He snapped on his overalls. He didn't bother with his underwear or shoes. Partly because he didn't have enough time, and partly because he wanted to be prepared if Cathy felt like fooling around after the ritual.

"Okay. Then I guess I'll just stay out of your way until you're finished."

He scooped her up in his arms. "You're never in the way."

"Y'know, Earl. You can make a girl almost glad she's dead."

"Almost?"

She shrugged. "Get me out of this cemetery, and we'll see."

"Got yourself a deal."

He knelt before the circle of runes. First, he burned the belladonna. Then he started the incantation, a long string of gibberish he'd had to spell out phonetically. When the time came, he sprinkled the dried raven's eye in the wind and incanted another segment of jabber. And on and on it went for about ten minutes. He'd chant and use something in the bag and chant some more and use something else in the bag. Very simple. Very redundant. Very boring.

Most of magic, particularly the ritual type of magic, was like that. A lot like clerical work, really. Sometimes you might spice it up with a little human sacrifice or maybe an orgy, but for the most part, if it was fun to do, it wasn't really necessary.

Most practitioners added superfluous elements to their magic just to spice things up, keep it interesting. It also helped to entertain the rubes that might make up a cult. He wasn't interested in any of that. This was just a bare-bones spell, and as he neared completion, his mind started wandering.

Earl wasn't much for romance, but he already had the whole evening planned out. He'd complete the ritual, sweep Cathy off her feet, and carry her from the graveyard like some great, dashing figure in a cliché-ridden love story. It always struck him as corny and a little unrealistic. Nobody lived happily ever after, even people who lived forever. But he was willing to pretend that they just might.

He traced a triangle in a circle in the dirt, raised his arms and launched into the final chant. It, at least, was in English.

"Oh, Kings of the Earth, Oh, Masters of the Spirit Realm, I call on you to hear my plea. Release this soul from your loving embrace so that she might freely roam the earth."

A green luminosity rose from the circle of salt, and the earth rumbled ever so lightly beneath him. He flashed a smile and a thumbs-up at Cathy.

"Those before her have departed and no longer need tending. Her task is done. Now I humbly ask you to discharge her from her sacred duties."

He reached to break the circle of salt as the final act of magic.

"Earl, is this supposed to happen?"

Cathy was fading away, and he hadn't even completed the spell. And she was right. It wasn't supposed to be happening. He forgot the ritual and ran to her. He tried to take her hands, but something was wrong. She wasn't quite solid anymore. He passed through her as if her flesh were thick motor oil.

She read the worry in his face. "What's wrong? What's going on?"

She faded, slipping through his fingers. He didn't know what to do to stop it.

"Don't go," he pleaded, knowing full well she had nothing to do with this.

Cathy dissolved into a barely visible cloud and then into nothing.

"Goddamn it!"

He flipped through his notepad, paced the circle, and cursed for a couple of minutes. He didn't even read the notes. He just glanced through them as if they might suddenly reveal the answer. They never did.

A gust swept through the cemetery. The candles extinguished, and the salt blew away. The dust swallowed up the runes.

"Son of a bitch!"

He tapped the pad against his temple, struggling to come up with an answer. There was only one. He'd screwed up. Something had gone wrong. He'd lost her. Maybe even killed her.

Earl's heart hammered at a thundering five beats a minute. He was too busy talking to himself to notice.

"Damn it! Don't panic, Earl. Stay calm. It's alright. Everything's alright. She's okay. She's not dead." He winced at the very thought and repeated the last phrase like a chant. "She's not dead. She's not dead. She's not dead."

Frustration overwhelmed him. He lashed out at a wooden grave marker. It snapped off and bounced away.

"Goddamn it, Earl, you stupid prick. C'mon and think." He stopped and forced himself to concentrate long enough to grab a coherent thought. "Hector! He'll know what to do. Yeah. He'll know."

He dashed out of the cemetery and toward the diner, repeating his mantra to keep sane. "She's not dead. She's not dead. She's not dead."

In the darkness of Make Out Barn, the old gods called to Tammy. This was nothing new. They'd always talked to her. Even before she'd stumbled across her destiny. She just hadn't known enough to understand them. But the way was opening, and what had once been a nagging whisper was now a thousand chattering voices. The old gods were close. Their time was near.

Tomorrow night.

Already their dimensional prison was weakening. Enough that they might infuse her, their final liberator, with a taste of the goddesshood that awaited her. There were side effects. The constant drone in her head made it hard to think. And something, many things actually, slithered around in her stomach.

The *Necronomicon* mentioned this. The old gods were ancient and powerful. Their energies mutated any human who invited them in. Not just physically, but mentally as well. No mortal could retain their reason under such exposure.

But with ultimate power, who needed sanity.

She lifted her Magic 8-Ball from the small mound of graveyard dirt. She turned over the black orb. The triangular thingamabob rose to the surface.

"Earl, where am I?"

She tossed the Magic 8-Ball in her backpack and removed the collection of exotic ingredients needed to create the Dust of Waking Sleep. She'd paid a hefty rush-delivery fee for her latest catalogue order and was pleased to find a plain, brown box waiting in her temple. Crazy Ctharl was not only reliable, but efficient to boot.

The dust would handle the mortals who opposed her. Assembling it herself saved her some money, even if it was more work. As for Duke, her latest shipment contained a jar of imps. And with all those obstacles put aside, Earl would be easy enough to stake during the day.

There was still one final problem. For the way to be opened, someone must be sacrificed. Getting a sacrifice was easy. But the sacrifice had to be performed by someone who "knew not what they did" according to her research. Paying someone to do it didn't count either. The higher forces weren't fooled by technicalities. She had to trick someone into it. There was always a catch. If these matters were easy, the old gods would not still be locked away.

Chad spoke up from the darkened corner where he huddled. "Mistress Lilith?"

Her head snapped around at the sudden noise, and he got a good, long look at her eyes. They were solid black. No white. No iris. Just inky darkness. He couldn't even be sure she had eyes anymore. Her sockets might very well have been empty.

"What, Chad?"

"Nuthin'."

She could smell his fear. It sent a quiver through her. She smiled, drawing in a deep, deep breath. She crawled toward him on her hands and knees.

"Does Big Jimmy need his lovin'?"

His heart beat faster as she drew closer. She could hear its thudding, feel its beating against his ribcage. The thought of scaring him to death only made her hungrier. She roughly shoved him on his back.

Tammy pushed away the power of the old gods. It wouldn't do to kill him just yet. Her eyes filled their sockets, but he was still scared. Just not scared enough to give up a chance to get laid.

After she'd finished with him, she realized just how mad she must have been to have actually enjoyed sex with Chad. But soon the voices returned, and she went back to work.

TWENTY-SIX

In the cramped quarters of the Magic 8-Ball, there was no room for Cathy's ectoplasmic body. She was reduced to a soul floating in murky, blue darkness. It was a lot like sitting in a warm bath way too long until the water got cold and your fingers were wrinkled and prunelike. Not that she had fingers, but there was still a general moistlike sensation in her disembodied spirit.

She was not alone.

"Who's there?"

Though she didn't speak with a voice, not using even ectoplasmic vocal cords, there was an echo. It lasted a long, long time, bouncing from one end of her prison to the other and back again. There was no reply, but she was certain there was somebody else here. She could just feel him.

"I know you're there."

Again, no answer.

She suddenly felt very claustrophobic. She had no form.

Space was currently a meaningless concept, but the other bodiless soul crowded around her. She could feel him. Her five senses were gone, replaced by a kind of spectral radar she hadn't quite adjusted to yet.

"I know you're there."

He laughed. A dry, humorless rasp that filled the dark and chilled her.

"Who's there?"

The specter's rough voice wormed its way into her immaterial guts.

"You know who I am, Cathy."

And she did. From somewhere other than herself the answer came.

"Gil Wilson?"

The name meant nothing to her. She'd never heard it before.

"That's right, dear Cathy."

"Where are we?"

"You already know that as well."

She did. From the same place she'd learned his name, more information came. They were bound within a Magic 8-Ball. Something had gone wrong, but it wasn't Earl's fault. Tammy had beaten him to the casting.

She didn't know who Tammy was, other than she didn't like her very much. In fact, she hated her. Despised her for the ungrateful, traitorous, little bitch she was. It was all very confusing.

"Our souls are mingled," Gil said. "A byproduct of the binding."

Bits and pieces of Gil Wilson filtered across her consciousness. They repulsed her. She wanted to get far away from him, but there was nowhere to go. She shrank into herself. He wrapped around her, his voice echoing from every direction.

"You can't fight it, Cathy. Your struggles only make it harder."

"Go away."

"I intend to. But first, I need your help."

More knowledge came to her.

She saw Gil poring over books, studying ancient texts, researching things man was never meant to know. Spending years and years in darkened rooms, deciphering arcane secrets, figuring heavenly alignments, and plowing deep into the advanced physics of interdimensional space until finally finding the fabled Gate of the Old Gods in a quiet, dusty town called Rockwood.

Coming to Rockwood, he'd bought the seemingly unremarkable plot of land under which the Gate rested and built a temple to his masters, disguised as an innocuous all-night diner. It was far more than that. Cathy saw how something that looked so ordinary could be so much more. It was all in the architecture, the angles, the placement of the supporting pillars, and all the other little details that added up to something wholly unnatural. Even the positioning of the porcelain toilets and track lighting made a difference. She didn't understand completely. She didn't want to. But she knew the diner served to weaken the Gate even further, and that this was not a good thing.

"Yes, Cathy, you know my secrets, and I know yours. I must admit I feel somewhat cheated by the exchange. I mean, really, the worst thing you ever did was lie about hitting a baseball into Mr. Weinberg's window."

He chuckled.

"Wait. I'm getting something else. Ah, you ran over a kitty once and stole some candy and also, yes, yes, you cheated on some math tests. Terrible sins indeed. The guilt must be tearing you apart."

The horrible acts Gil Wilson had performed in his quest for unholy power swam just beneath her own memories. In an effort to repulse them, she concentrated on the less ghastly remembrances invading her.

Strongest was the night fate, or destiny, or perhaps merely random chance had nearly destroyed his chances for godhood. It was after a simple ritual, the final consecration rite of his temple. After sanctifying it with an offering of his own blood, he rose on wobbly legs. Groggy from the magic spell, he failed to notice a ketchup bottle lying on the floor.

It fell underfoot, and he tripped. The knife wound up between him and the tile. It plunged into his heart.

The old gods, enraged at his failure, gathered up enough power to reach out and drag him to their hell where they might torment him for eternity. They only got his flesh. His spirit barely slipped through their grasp. But as a ghost, Gil was powerless to open the way.

He'd all but given up hope when finally stumbling upon Tammy. Sensing the talent within her, he groomed her to complete what he had started. When she opened the way, the old gods would know who was really responsible for their rise and reward him appropriately.

He'd tutored her, teaching her secrets only he knew. She'd locked him in this prison in gratitude. Where he could once again feel his destiny passing him by. Yet fate saw fit to give him another chance. By persuading Tammy to bind another ghost in the ball, he'd tricked her into giving him his means of escape.

"That's right," he agreed. "Together, we are strong. Strong enough to escape this prison."

"No."

His voice became icy. "What?"

"No!" she repeated, stronger than before. "I won't help you. You belong here. I won't let you out."

"Would you stay with me then? For eternity?"

She didn't want to. His soul was like acid, eating away at her own spirit. But he was too dangerous, even as a ghost, to let loose on the world. Even if it did end up destroying her utterly.

"How selfless," Gil spat, as if through clenched teeth. "Yours is a noble soul, girl, but I will not be denied."

She tucked deeper into herself, calling upon fond memories in an effort to ignore him. Playing baseball with her dad. Her favorite song. Her college graduation. Earl.

"Your undead admirer. You are quite fond of him, aren't you?" Gil's voice oozed into her. "In fact, you love him. A trifle premature, if you'd like my opinion. You haven't even known him a week."

"Shut up!" She wished she had hands to cover her immaterial ears. "Leave him out of this!"

"You'll never see him again, shut away in this ball, Cathy."

"I don't care!"

"Yes, you do." He thrust deeper, digging into her memories. "Cathy, you little slut. Throwing yourself at the first vampire that comes along. I'm disappointed in you."

She didn't want to remember, but he forced her to.

"You'll never feel his touch again. You'll never feel anything again. Just you and me together for eternity. Or you can help me, free yourself, and run away with Earl."

It wasn't as simple as that. If she let him out, then the world would end. There'd be no place for Earl and her to run away to.

"But if you keep me here, Tammy shall complete the ceremony anyway. It's your choice. I can't force you. Either way, the world ends. At least my way, you'll get to spend a few precious hours with your lover. Who knows? You might even warn him in enough time to stop me." He laughed skeptically. "Doubtful, but you're welcome to try."

She groped for other solutions, but none came. This was the only way. The only way to save the world. The only way to save Earl. And she admitted to herself that he was her true reason for even considering it. She'd been alone too long. Whether it was selfish or not, she had to take the chance.

"Okay, what do I have to do?"

"Not yet. Tammy is watching. But soon."

In the darkness of their prison, Gil Wilson grinned a wide, immaterial smile.

"Soon."

TWENTY-SEVEN

Earl spent the rest of the night in the empty graveyard. Hector hadn't been able to provide any answers for what had happened. He reassured Earl he'd look into it, but Earl didn't have much hope. He sat on Cathy's grave, nursing a six-pack, and feeling sorry for himself. It was times like this that he really missed being able to get drunk.

About half-an-hour before dawn, Duke moseyed into the cemetery.

"I'd offer you a beer, but this is my last one." Earl popped it open. The warm alcohol foamed and spilled over his hands. "Shit."

"Hector tell you what happened?" Duke asked.

"Nope. Said she might have finally moved on to the next plane."

"Say why?"

"Said he didn't know, but told me he didn't see how it could've been anything I'd done."

Earl offered Duke a drink. Duke waved it away.

"No thanks. So how you doing?"

"Me? I'm just fine. I just killed my girlfriend, that's all. How else should I be?"

"If Hector said it ain't your fault, then it ain't."

"Aw that's bullshit. I screwed it up, Duke. She was the best thing that ever happened to me, and I screwed it up."

Earl threw the half-full aluminum can at the moon. It twirled, spraying beer, and hung in the air for a long while before finally coming down to earth.

"I fucked it all up."

"Ain't as bad as all that," Duke offered.

"Hell it ain't!"

Earl wiped a solitary drop of moisture that had managed to work its way free of his dried-up tear ducts.

"Sorry, Duke. I ain't mad at you, but you just don't understand. You don't know what it's like, being me. Everybody likes you. Or at least they don't not like you."

"People like you, Earl."

"No, people get used to me." He chuckled. "It's not the same thing. No big deal, really. I'm used to it. My mama didn't even like me. And my daddy thought I was a worthless pile of cow shit. Told me so on his deathbed. Pulled me over and whispered it in my ear just before croaking.

"My whole life, I can count four people who liked me. There's you, and this pet turtle I had when I was six, and my grammy Betta. And Cathy. She was the first woman who really liked me."

"There'll be others."

"You aren't listening to me. I'm ninety-seven years old.

Ninety-seven. That's almost a whole damn century on this earth. And all I got to show for it are four people. And one of them ain't even a person.

"I used'ta wonder sometimes why living forever was supposed to be a good thing. Don't get me wrong. Being immortal ain't all that bad. I was always a night person anyway, and the powers can be kind'a cool. But, I mean, this whole undead stuff sounds good on paper, but it ain't all it's cracked up to be.

"See, the way I got it figured, dying is sort'a like the thing that gives your life meaning. You may not want to get there, but, without it, you're just looking at a long, long road to nowhere. I'd gotten used to looking down that road, Duke." He looked to the horizon where the sun would be rising soon. "But I don't think I can do it anymore."

"What'cha talking about, Earl?"

"I'm talking 'bout maybe it's time to end it."

Duke cast a disagreeable glance at the vampire.

"Now hear me out 'fore calling me stupid. Everybody's gotta die. We undead try to pretend like we don't, but just 'cuz we don't die of natural causes, that ain't exactly the same thing. Sure, it's possible I might last till the end of time, but I wouldn't take odds on that.

"Now I've lived a good hundred years. Most of it hasn't been bad. There's been some good spots here and there, but mostly it was a whole lotta nuthin' special. Then Cathy and these last five days come along, and I figure that it was worth the wait. And it was. But now that it's over, I don't think there's anything better out there waiting for me.

"Now I'm not saying I really want to kill myself. But it's gonna happen eventually, and either I'll have to do it myself or somebody's gonna do it for me. Probably in one of the less pleasant ways."

"What's your point?"

"Point is, Duke, one way or another, I'm gonna die tonight. And I'm asking you, as my best friend, to help me out. I'll just turn my back, here on Cathy's grave, and think about her, and you'll sneak up right behind me, and rip my head clean off. It'll be the last favor I ever ask you, and if you're really my friend, you'll do it for me."

He turned, cleared his head, and felt the cold, dry earth beneath him. Cathy's smiling face came to him, and he smiled back at her. He dared hope that he'd find her on the other side, though if there was an afterlife, he doubted they'd end up in the same place.

"You aren't gonna do it, are you?"

Duke shook his head.

"Damn it, you prick. It ain't all that much to ask."

"Maybe, but you'll have to do it yourself."

"Fine. I will. I'll just let the sun take care of it."

"You do that." Duke hocked up a mouthful of saliva and mucus and spat it in the dirt. "Y'know, Earl, there'll be others."

"Not like her."

"Give it time."

"What? Another hundred years? Thanks, but no thanks."

"Suit yourself. You ever seen a vampire done in by sunlight?"

"No."

"I have. Once." Duke shook his head slowly. "It's not like in the movies. He didn't blow up or catch fire or nuthin' quick like that. No, it was more like he turned to sludge. First his skin peeled off, layer by layer. Then his muscles sorta just sloshed off his bones. And his organs smoldered and dripped into a black puddle. Then his bones popped and snapped and liquefied. Took 'bout five minutes for the poor bastard to finally expire. He screamed himself hoarse for most of it."

Earl glared. "You aren't talking me out of this, Duke."

"I'm not trying to. Just figured I'd tell you what you had to look forward to."

"Thanks."

"You're welcome. Well, you got about ten minutes to dawn. I'd stick around but seeing one bloodsucker get a tan was enough for me."

"If you were my friend, you'd kill me."

"Well, maybe I'll feel up to it tomorrow night, but you can't wait that long." As the werewolf walked through the cemetery gates, he shouted without looking back. "See you 'round, Earl . . . or I guess not."

The first rays of dawn came. The horizon turned soft red. It hurt Earl's eyes to look at it. He tried thinking of Cathy, to not think about the pain morning might inflict on his delicate complexion.

"Damn it, Duke," he grumbled. "You better kill me tomorrow, or I'll have'ta kick your ass, you son of a bitch." Squinting, he shielded his eyes and ran back to the diner.

TWENTY-EIGHT

As the sun rose, a drowsiness fell upon Earl. It took forty-five minutes for his undead nature to overtake his stressed mind. His sleep was restless. Normally he lay in his steamer in a corpselike slumber, but today, he twitched and kicked. Headless Napoleon sat curled up on his chest.

Duke checked on him a couple of times the first hour, and a couple of times the next hour as well.

"You really care about him," Loretta observed.

He closed the trunk and rapped it softly with his knuckles. "He needs looking after."

"S'pose he does at that. Seems to be taking things pretty hard. He's lucky to have a friend like you."

"Guess so, but it ain't a one way thing. He's been there for me when nobody else was. Sure am gonna miss him if he don't change his mind."

" 'Bout leaving?"

Duke sat on the steamer. Snorting, he wrung his hands. "Wants me to kill him."

Loretta gaped. "Over a missing ghost?"

"Mostly. But you gotta understand, life ain't exactly been easy for him. Being undead doesn't help none."

"We all got our troubles, Duke."

"True enough," he agreed. "But he made a good case for himself. I don't really see as I got much of a choice."

"Good Lord says there's always a choice."

"Don't know if Earl and the Good Lord are on speaking terms. Anyway, if he still wants it tonight, I'll have to do it."

"You can't."

"Gotta. I'm his best friend."

"I'll pray for him."

"Don't know if that'll help, but I appreciate the effort just the same."

Duke spent the rest of the morning finishing the diner's new gas line. The job was mostly done, but he took his time. It kept his mind off zombies, old gods, haunted diners, and suicidal vampires. For the moment, none of those problems existed. There was only the trench and the pipe. Duke didn't care much for hard labor. He didn't dislike it. It was just something to do, usually for money and occasionally for distraction. And though he stretched this particular distraction out as long as he could, it inevitably came to an end. He tossed the last shovelful of dirt back into place and smoothed it with the rusty spade.

He caught Tammy's scent a moment before she spoke up.

"Nice job."

"Thanks."

She slid behind him, pressing her body against his, looping her hands around his wide waist as much as she was able.

He pulled away.

"What's a matter, Duke," she purred. "Don't you like girls?"

He drove the shovel into the hard ground. "I like women."

"Oh, c'mon." She glided closer. "I know you want me."

He put his hands on her shoulders, careful to keep to a minimal, fingers-only contact. No palms. "Tammy, it ain't gonna happen." He gently, but firmly pushed her away.

She stuck out her lower lip. "Why not? You like me. I like you."

" 'Cuz it isn't that simple."

"Yes, it is."

She batted her eyelashes and ran her hand down her midriff.

The primal forces that shared Duke's soul agreed. They wanted nothing more than to throw Tammy to the ground, to feel the warmth of her skin, to watch the sweat bead on her breasts, and make her moan and grunt and tremble beneath the hot, desert sun. Another time, another place, he wouldn't have hesitated, but a couple thousand years of civilization stood between him and that place. Not that the werewolf in him gave half-a-damn about any of that. But the man did, and it was every bit as stubborn as the beast.

"Whatever," she sighed. "Loretta told me to tell you she wants a word with you."

They went inside. He found Loretta in the kitchen, standing at the grill with her back to them. He grunted to announce his entrance. She turned slowly. Gray, chalky powder covered her blank face.

He whirled on the petite girl. "It's you."

"Took you long enough to figure it out."

She threw a small vial at his feet. It shattered, releasing a thousand impish demons into the kitchen. The swirling flock of greens, browns, and reds covered him in a buzzing, chattering swarm. The imps were only the size of horseflies, but they held him in place. Calling upon every ounce of strength, he lurched forward one step.

In the diner, the voices of the old gods were overwhelming. Tammy's eyes darkened to black holes. She grabbed a rolling pin from the counter and spun it lazily.

Duke pushed forward another six inches. Imps screamed and expired in smoky puffs.

Tammy grinned. Her mouth stretched wider than her face would allow, and her cheeks spread to compensate. "You blew it, Duke. I would've screwed your brains out. Well, I guess I can't have everything. Not yet, anyway."

Duke's right forearm broke free. Some imps exploded. Others were thrown across the kitchen. Duke crushed a couple underfoot with another struggling stomp.

Tammy let the pin go. Instead of falling, it hovered in the air. She rotated her finger clockwise. The pin spun slowly. She wiggled a second finger, and it became a whirling blur about her head.

"I don't really want to do this, Duke. So why don't you be a good boy and stop struggling. Otherwise, I'll have to hurt you." She clapped. The wooden pin zipped forward and struck a glancing blow off his brow. "I like you. Don't make me kill you."

Duke's body tightened. Imps popped in droves in the losing fight to hold him back.

"Have it your way."

The rolling pin flitted about almost too fast to follow, smashing in Duke's skull over and over again. Bone crunched beneath wood. He stood against the barrage far better than a mere mortal. It took a full minute for his knees to buckle. Then another minute to get him on the floor. Even after he stopped moving, blood pooling around his cracked head, Tammy had the pin strike another dozen blows. Just to be on the safe side. The glistening red club rolled about in small circles.

"Can I use your phone?" Tammy asked.

Loretta stared into space, seemingly unaware of the bloody mess in her kitchen. She was actually quite aware, but the Dust of Waking Sleep prevented her from doing anything about it.

Tammy pinched Loretta's cheek. "Thanks."

She called Chad to tell him she'd be needing him tonight. He offered up a lame excuse about needing to finish an English report. The dumbass was losing his nerve. She wasn't surprised, but he was essential to her plans. She couldn't have a sacrifice without a victim. Rather than explain that to him, she told him that if he didn't show up by six, she'd be very unhappy, and all the very nasty things a high priestess of the old gods could do when she got very unhappy. That was enough to convince him.

It wasn't hard to find Earl's trunk. He lay in twitching sleep. Napoleon raised his half-face and growled at her. He couldn't stop her from pounding a stake into the vampire's heart. Earl's eyelids fluttered open and a weak gasp escaped his throat.

Tammy spent a couple of minutes debating whether to finish him off. She decided to keep him around just in case Duke failed to perform as she expected. It was always handy to have a backup plan.

She went back into the kitchen and had a seat beside Duke's carcass. Napoleon trailed, barking and yipping at her ankles. She tried ignoring him, but her patience waned. She threw a bolt of spectral lightning at the dog. He whined and ran off.

"Y'know, Loretta, I didn't want to do it this way. I didn't want to reveal myself. It's a risk I'd rather not have taken. But you had to be stubborn about this. You couldn't just leave."

The old gods stared up through the thick, red pool. The blood boiled with their impatience.

Duke moaned. His fingers jerked.

"Stubborn, stubborn, stubborn."

A cast-iron skillet joined the rolling pin in a new round of werewolf-braining.

TWENTY-NINE

Tammy's mother avoided going into her daughter's room if she could help it. She wasn't the snooping kind. Not that she trusted her daughter. She often got the impression that Tammy was not a nice girl, that there were darker things lurking just behind her eyes. But Tammy's mother also believed that it was her duty to ignore these hunches. Her job was to nurture and care. It was the father's responsibility to address the unpleasant business of the teenage years. Unmentionable female-related bits the exception. But twice a week it was required of her as a good mother to venture into Tammy's room and collect the small pile of dirty laundry stacked by the door.

She diligently avoided looking at anything else lying about the bedroom. She didn't notice the Magic 8-Ball on the dresser, and her back was turned as it started throbbing like a living thing. She gathered up the dirty clothes, blissfully unaware of the incredible spiritual forces being brought to bear mere feet away. At the exact moment she left, shutting the door behind her, the ball split in two and fell to the floor with a muted thump against the carpet. The liquid spilled, forming a deep blue stain that would greatly displease Tammy's mother when she discovered it.

An ectoplasmic cloud billowed from the broken orb. Four eyes formed. Eight tangled limbs solidified. The mist split as the very different souls of Cathy and Gil Wilson repulsed each other. It was a natural aversion, like oil and water. It was also very draining, spiritually speaking. Cathy's legs weren't up to supporting her just yet. She floated until she noticed her feet weren't touching the ground. Flesh-and-blood people didn't defy gravity, and Cathy fell on her butt with a resurgence of mortal expectation.

Most of Gil Wilson had left her, but there were bits left behind: nuggets of information about ghostly existence. Ectoplasm was a product of the soul, and as such reacted mostly how the soul expected it to. It was why ghosts tended to look as they did in life, and why their intangible form didn't just sink into the earth or float away. Knowing that didn't make it any easier to change her instinctive reactions, but at least now she understood why it happened.

The rot in Gil Wilson's soul manifested in a sallow, wasted form. His flesh was peeling, muscle and bone showing beneath. An ectoplasmic duplicate of the sacrificial dagger that had killed him stuck out of his chest. He grinned with long and sharp teeth. He stretched, first his arms, then his legs, and finally his head, which he twisted nearly three-hundred-and-sixty degrees with a pop and a crack.

"You'll only get this warning once, girl. Fuck with me, and I'll spend the next thousand years tormenting you in ways the living can't imagine. Your soul shall be a shattered, wasted thing when I'm through with it. Are we perfectly clear?"

Standing, she nodded.

"Why don't I believe you?"

She backed away. "I won't. I swear."

"Don't bother lying, Cathy. I've seen your soul. You're too decent, too damn good. Even now I know what's running through your mind. You're thinking of Earl, and how you can't just leave him there to face Tammy by himself. If it makes you feel any better, I can assure you he's dead by now."

He sneered. "Shit. You're too much a Goddamn Goodie Two-shoes. Better to send you off to final death than take the chance when I'm so close."

Ghosts couldn't normally harm ghosts. Ectoplasm was resilient stuff. But Gil Wilson was no ordinary spirit. He pulled the dagger from his chest. The black blade radiated darkness. His form distorted as if reflected in a fun house mirror. Limbs snaked toward her.

Her only chance was to run for it. The tentacle that had been Gil's foot looped around her ankle. She fell. He dragged her toward him, slowly and deliberately, reveling in her helplessness.

"Cooperate, girl, and I'll make this quick. Well, not *too* quick."

Cathy dug her fingers in the floor. It didn't help. The shapeless, oily cloud hovered over her. He sliced down her back with the dagger. It was a shallow cut, just deep enough to allow some of her soul seep away. A tiny piece of her evaporated into the ether. She screamed. It wasn't just the pain. It was the horrible realization that a part of her was gone forever.

Gil flipped her over to watch her writhe in agony. "It's been a long time since I've gotten a chance to do this, Cathy. I'd forgotten how much fun it was."

He wasn't going to just kill her. He was going to deliver her into final death one scrap of soul at a time. He sliced open her cheek and inhaled the escaping wisps.

"Hmmm. I wonder what that was. Perhaps a cherished memory of first love. Or your disgustingly overdeveloped compassion? Maybe even those precious moments playing baseball with your father. Never did learn to hit those curveballs, did you?"

A fragment of hope came to her. He had a knife, a copy of something important enough in life to warrant ghostly reproduction. She closed her eyes and remembered the bat she'd spent countless hours swinging in her backyard. It'd been years since she'd held it, but it was something she could never forget. Indulging himself in her suffering, Gil Wilson didn't notice the spectral bat materialize in her hands.

She swung with as much force as she could muster from the floor. His body deformed with the blow. He rolled off her with a growl.

"Well, I'll be damned, Cathy. You seem to have picked up a few tricks from our mingling. I'm impressed."

She adopted a batting stance. "Get the fuck away from me!"

"How very frightening," he cooed. "That weapon really can't hurt me. It's not that sort of memory. And besides that, you don't have it in you." He raised the dagger and slipped forward.

She swung again. The blow connected with the quasi-solid goo of his ectoplasm. He wobbled, dropping the dagger.

"You're really starting to piss me off!" he rumbled.

Cathy brought the bat down. His body crashed apart into a gray slime. It struggled to reshape itself. A lump with eyes rose up, only to be pounded back down. The slime bubbled as Gil tried to regain his senses. She smacked him again, but she was only keeping him down. He was right. She couldn't kill him. Not with her bat.

She snatched up the dagger beside her. The blade sent cold shivers up her arm. It was more than just a knife. It was every depravity of Gil Wilson's damned soul given form.

"Go ahead," Gil said. "You know you want to."

Another voice came to her. "You've got no choice. It's either you or him. Do it."

She hesitated.

"He should be dead. You're just correcting a mistake."

It made sense, but she'd never killed anyone before. Even if he did deserve it, she wasn't sure she could. But she had to. She tightened her grip on the dagger. It bit into her palm, eager to kill anyone, even its own creator.

Cathy glanced at her arm. Her flesh was graying and shriveling. Using the knife, no matter how much she should, would blacken her soul and maybe send her down the path Gil Wilson had taken.

The blade screamed. "Do it!"

She threw it away. It clattered a few feet away.

A fist erupted from the puddle of Gil Wilson. Cathy was knocked away. The goo rose and hovered in the air. The dagger jumped into his hand. Cathy held up her bat, preparing to defend herself.

"Much as I'd like to continue," he sighed, "I must be off.

We'll have to finish this some other time. After I've become a god."

He turned and vanished through the far bedroom wall. After ten minutes, Cathy was finally convinced he'd left and dropped her guard. She sat on the bed and wrung her baseball bat nervously. She wanted to run away, but when the old gods returned, even earthbound spirits would be at their mercy. And she couldn't leave Earl. Even if he was probably dead by now.

She prayed he wasn't. Not just because she cared for him. Without some help in the physical world, a spirit didn't stand a ghost of a chance of stopping Tammy from opening the way.

THIRTY

Chad had no doubts. He most definitely did not want the old gods to rise tonight. While the world he knew was not all to his liking, something told him it beat the hell out of the remade one Tammy kept telling him about. He knew she couldn't be talked out of it, and he wanted to be on the right side of the world's new masters. And he was afraid of Tammy. More terrified of her than even the inscrutable and thoroughly inhuman powers she served. The fear made him obey her. That, along with a dash of waning teenage lust and leftover particles of puppy love.

But it was mostly fear.

His apprehension only grew when he saw the police cruiser in the diner lot. He parked beside it and went inside with slow, reluctant steps.

Tammy and Sheriff Kopp stood in the middle of the dining area. She smiled and bound to his side.

"There you are. I was beginning to think you weren't going

to make it." She took his hands and kissed him on the cheek. She led him back toward Sheriff Kopp with a skipping gait.

The sheriff tipped his hat at Chad. Chad flashed a nervous grin and swallowed a lump in his throat.

"The sheriff was just explaining to me how he might finally have a handle on all the trouble Loretta's been having," Tammy chirped.

"Really?" Chad mumbled. He felt uncomfortably warm.

"Oh, yes. Go ahead and tell him, Sheriff."

"That's alright," Kopp said. "I really just wanted to speak with Loretta. Is she in back?"

"I think so."

Chad's legs trembled. He fell into a chair.

Kopp headed toward the kitchen. Tammy ruffled around in her backpack. "Oh, it's very interesting how he did it. See, he figured that there was some sort of magical spell interfering with his perception, and that if he stopped and forced himself to really think about it, he just might able to break the influence. So he spent all this afternoon just thinking and thinking about it. And finally it came to him. Make Out Barn."

She sprinkled some powder from a pouch into her palm.

"It all makes perfect sense really. Remember how everyone used to hang out there, Chad. Then there was that fire, and everybody just sort of stayed away." She giggled. "Almost like magic."

Kopp passed into the kitchen. The swinging doors swished back and forth four times, and he emerged, pistol in hand.

"Tammy, Chad, you're under arrest."

She grinned. He'd finally broken the spell of muddling. It was only a matter of time. Once he'd found her temple, he'd soon remember the graveyard incident she'd tucked into his un-conscious. The mess in the kitchen was merely the final straw.

Chad jumped, hands in air.

"Oh come now," Tammy said. "You won't shoot us. We're just kids."

Kopp eased back the hammer on his revolver. "I'm not go-ing to tell you again. I don't want to shoot you."

Her silky black hair squirmed about her shoulders as if it were alive. "Go ahead. You can't stop me now. Not with bullets anyway. Not here. Not now."

The sheriff fired. The shot thundered in Chad's ears. He shut his eyes tight and held them shut with bated breath. He wasn't sure if he wanted Tammy dead or not. He dared open one eye and saw the bullet hovering mere inches from Tammy's face. The projectile spun, suspended in the air.

"Too little, too late."

She threw out her handful of dust. It shot across the room and hit Sheriff Kopp in the face. He sputtered and coughed before slumping into a relaxed posture. The gun slipped from his fingers and fell to the tile.

Tammy plucked the dangling bullet from the air. Chuck-ling, she tossed it away. Invisible forces lowered the window blinds. The front door locked all by itself.

"Come along, Chad. We've got work to do."

Chad followed her into the back where Duke lay in a puddle of blood. Duke's head was dented. Hair had been stripped away in some spots, showing skull and maybe even brains. Chad didn't look too close for fear of losing his lunch.

"You killed him."

"Your point?" she asked.

He glanced up at the ceiling to avoid seeing corpse brain or her creepy, empty eyes. Up to now, Tammy hadn't killed anyone. She'd talked about it a lot, but this was the first fresh dead guy he'd seen. His stomach churned.

"He's only temporarily dead, anyway," she sighed. "We need him for the final sacrifice."

Chad risked another glance at Duke's body. It was hard believe he wasn't well and truly deceased. Even if he were a werewolf, it seemed leaking brains should kill just about anybody.

He noticed Loretta for the first time. She was easy to ignore, just standing in the corner. That same chalky powder Tammy had thrown on the sheriff covered her face. At least she wasn't dead. Not yet, anyway.

Tammy grabbed Duke by a leg. "Help me move this guy, dumbass."

The urge to bolt rose within him, but her stare compelled him to obey. Gripping the corpse's other leg, he allowed his mind to shut off. His body switched to autopilot. She told him what to do, and he did it without really thinking about it. It was either that, or huddle in the corner and wet himself.

Dragging Duke to the front was no easy feat. He weighed a ton. Chad stared at the trail of red left behind. They were really going to do it. They were going to raise the old gods and end the world. The part of his mind still working found it strange that it could all end so easily. There wasn't all that much to it. According to Tammy, the diner did most the work. She just had to charge it up with some basic chanting and black-magic-type stuff and sacrifice someone at the right moment. The Gate would be thrown wide, and mankind would be swallowed whole by a gushing tide of horrors.

"Bummer," the little piece of his soul still functioning re-marked.

"Uh, Mistress Lilith, what about him?" He pointed to the sheriff.

"What about him?"

"Is he alright?"

"For the moment."

"He's just gonna stand there and watch us?"

"Yeah? So? If he bothers you so much why don't you take him to the kitchen. I'm busy. And why don't you stay in there until I need you, too."

Chad was only too eager to comply. Kopp and Loretta and all the blood bothered him, but not nearly so much as Tammy.

He briefly wondered where Earl was and decided he'd rather not know. Then he sat quietly and thought about all the action he'd gotten out of this deal. Somewhere along the way, he decided it had been worth it. It was only too bad he couldn't get one more jump in before the end.

THIRTY-ONE

The diner didn't need much help in its sacred task. It had been leeching the supernatural energies of the Gate for years now. All that unnatural potential had to go somewhere. Weird shit attracts more weird shit, and this mother lode of strangeness had no small effect on Rockwood. Under the influence of the Gate, the small town had suffered a veritable invisible plague of otherworldly afflictions. Not that the plague was all that invisible. Just mostly unnoticed through supernatural influence.

Even now, the upswing of power was having its way with this rural patch of desert. The sun hadn't even set, and already darkness was descending. There would be no stars tonight. The population of Rockwood would cower in their homes, stricken with an unexplainable apprehension. The werewolf, who would normally stay dead a good twenty-four hours given the time and method of his demise, was already recovering nicely. His broken skull was knitting itself together so that within a few hours, he'd be back on his feet. Just in time to provide the old gods with their sacrifice.

In the meantime, Tammy performed what little preparations needed to be made. The eternal stain on the floor, the ill-fated final offering of Gil Wilson, boiled and steamed. She dipped her fingers in the crimson pool and used the dark powers within to paint her runes. She set up a few candles in key points of power. She read through chants she had already memorized long ago. And she waited for the hour of the opening.

At some point, the ghost of Gil Wilson showed up.

"How did you get out?" she asked.

"You didn't think to hold me forever, did you?"

She had hoped, but she was not at all surprised. Gil Wilson was no ordinary specter. She didn't have time to bother with him at the moment.

"You need to add a little line here." He indicated a half-finished rune.

"I know," she snapped.

"And that candle over there should be a few more inches to the left."

"I don't think so."

"This is my design, girl. You're merely a pair of hands to finish what I started. Fix the candle."

Her hands tightened into fists. Distant thunder rumbled. "It doesn't need fixing."

Gil Wilson despised his situation. She'd learned the forbidden arts well, but she was still merely an amateur. Her level of magical powers paled to those he'd possessed while alive, but being dead put him at a disadvantage. Though he knew of ways to kill even from the ectoplasmic sphere, he couldn't do it. Not when his plans were so close to fruition.

"Fine. Leave the candle. It won't make much difference anyway."

And it wouldn't. Just a little hiccup in the cross-dimensional matrix. Yet, the very idea annoyed him. Any Armageddon worth doing was worth doing right. When she wasn't looking, he edged over and gave the errant candle a spectral nudge in the right direction. Tammy blasted him with a spirit bolt. His body collapsed into a puddle of blackened ectoplasm.

She calmly readjusted the candle. "I know what I'm doing. Now go and sit in the corner before I splatter you all over your precious diner."

He conceded, slithering into a booth.

The sun set, and a smothering black rolled up like ebony fog. It was almost as if the whole of Creation had vanished. That if one stepped out the door of Gil's All Night Diner, they'd tumble into oblivion. The only light at all came from the moon. The glowing crescent cast down a hard glare that shone upon the diner like a spotlight. As it rose, it grew brighter and fuller. And larger, as if drawing closer and closer to the earth, pulled downward by the unnatural collapse of space. The light filtered through the windows, bending and arcing in ways that defied physics, shining on hideous faces shimmering in the air through the thinning dimensional veil.

Time dragged. Tammy grew impatient. The old gods grew impatient. They filled her mind with hideous growls and shrieks, but when the time of the casting finally drew near, half past seven-thirty, they quieted down to allow her to concentrate.

She called Chad in, performed some last minute checks, and began.

She handed her follower a large knife. "When the moon is full and the sky is red, you have to plunge this in Duke's heart."

"Me?" He held the knife away from him in two awkward hands. "But I haven't ever, uhmm, well, why can't you do it?"

"Because you have to."

"But—"

"But what?" She put both hands on his neck and squeezed with delicate, impossibly strong fingers. "Did you think you could earn the favor of the old gods without shedding blood?"

"Uh . . . well."

"Did you think you could ascend to godhood without first proving yourself?" She chuckled. "You stupid son of a bitch. There's no such thing as a free ride."

"But . . ."

She pulled him close. Her breath smelled of rot.

"You'll kill him, Chad. It's a great responsibility. The final sacrifice. I know you won't let me down."

"No, Mistress Lilith," he gasped.

"That's my boy."

She let him go and began the Incantation of Reborn Darkness in a quiet mumble.

The knife trembled in Chad's hands. He glanced from the blade to the moon to Duke's body. Something sinister bubbled up in his brain. It was the chorus of hell, and he surrendered to it. It swallowed his conscience and doubts, leaving him with a numb indifference. The moon ascended. Shadows slipped across its face as it grew bigger.

Tammy chanted in ever-increasing volume.

". . . And the sacrifice shall be made by one who knows not what he does, and the blood shall wash away the Fetters of Ages. The Gate shall swing wide, and Frush'ee'aghov the Lesser shall be the first. And he shall open his eye and behold the world. In beholding it, he shall unmake the cursed guardians of light. And the old gods will step onto the Earth, and the blight of man shall be wiped away."

Her voice echoed deep and long. Shapes squirmed beneath the floor like malformed sharks swimming just below the surface. Chad held the knife over his head and watched the moon.

"Ee-Thay age-ay of-ay ight-lay ill-way end-ay oonight-tay. Frush'ee'aghov, eye-ay offer-ay ee-thay is-thay aste-tay of-ay udd-blay at-thay ou-yay ite-may eepare-pray ee-thay orld-way oo-tay eceeve-ray or-yay others-bray."

Chad's muscles tightened to deliver the deathblow.

Duke twitched. His head was practically healed, but Chad didn't dare strike before the sign was given.

Tammy kept chanting. Her masters joined in, filling the diner with a thousand inhuman voices. The very earth grumbled beneath them.

A red haze crept across the moon's twisted face.

Cathy pushed her way through the dark soup of the last night. The closer she got to the diner, the more resistance her ectoplasm met—as if the old gods knew her intent and were trying to keep her away. She pushed on, even when she couldn't see anything at all. As long as it kept getting harder, she figured it had to be the right direction. Just when she thought it would become too thick to continue, she broke through.

The diner pulsed and throbbed. Hundreds of bestial spirits wormed their way from the concrete walls and gathered in a gray cloud made of screaming, twisted grimaces.

She bit back the urge to run shrieking into the night and peeked through the large front window. Knife in hand, Chad stood over Duke's body. Tammy chanted. Gil Wilson watched on. There was no sign of Earl.

"Crap."

With Gil around, she needed protection. Her phantom baseball bat materialized in her hands again. She went around and walked through the back wall. The pool of Duke's blood rumbled and growled. Loretta and Sheriff Kopp stood to one side.

Tammy's chant roared from the front.

"Eyes-ray! Eyes-ray! Eyes-ray! Frush'ee'aghov, Frush'ee 'aghov, Frush'ee'aghov! Eyes-ray! Eye-ay ive-gay ee-thay urld-way oo-tay oo-yay! Eyes-ray!"

The diner slurped down Duke's blood through a pinhole interdimensional drain in the floor. A disfigured limb, part hand, part hoof, forced its way upward.

Something growled from behind Cathy. Then it yipped excitedly.

"Napoleon!" The dog jumped in her arms. Half his head was missing, but she had more pressing problems.

"Where's Earl, boy? Where's Earl?"

Napoleon lapped at her face with half of a wet tongue.

"I'm glad to see you, too, boy, but where's Earl? I have to find Earl."

The ghostly terrier wagged his tail enthusiastically.

"Never mind. I'll find him myself."

She let him down. He circled her legs as she went to the

storeroom. Earl lay in an open steamer trunk. She set down her bat and grabbed the stake in his chest. "Come on, Earl. I need you. The world needs you."

An ectoplasmic tentacle wrapped her neck and yanked her away. "I thought I heard something," Gil Wilson remarked. "Cathy, you foolish, foolish girl. I guess I'll have to kill you."

He knocked away her bat as she reached for it. She tried to pry off his choke-hold. He squeezed. The pressure was about to pop her head off her shoulders when Napoleon bit into Gil Wilson's butt. Gil yelped. Cathy slipped free and grabbed her bat.

Gil twisted and growled at the terrier attached to his rear end. Napoleon dug in deeper.

Cathy took advantage of the distraction to awaken Earl. She yanked, and the stake came halfway out.

Napoleon howled as Gil Wilson's arm distorted and sliced off his tail. The dog lost hold and fell away, whining.

"Fucking mutt!"

Cathy raised her bat to fend him off, but his arm snaked in an odd angle and knocked her down. She tumbled back. The stake arced through the air and bounced off a can of tomato soup. He was too intent on killing her to notice.

"Did you really think you could stop this from happening, you bitch? Are you really that stupid? Goddamn if I can understand what was going through that mind of yours. No matter. I'll enjoy killing you." He grinned. "And your little dog, too."

His gleaming dagger literally sliced through the air. Evil spirits slipped through the gash and flew up and away.

"Get the hell away from my girlfriend!"

Earl threw his arms around the specter. He opened his

mouth wider than humanly possible and sank long, white fangs into Gil Wilson's neck, or the best possible approximation given the ghost's current blob-like shape.

The ghost screeched as Earl slurped down his soul. It burned his throat and seared his stomach, but he choked it down. It was the only way for a vampire to kill a ghost. Wilson tried to ooze away but escape was impossible once the fangs were in. He could only bluster and flail while his ectoplasmic form dissolved.

"This is my destiny! Nothing can stop me! Nothing! Not even death!"

Earl inhaled the last of Gil Wilson. He grimaced and spat. "Goddamn that guy tasted like shit." He lifted Cathy in a tight embrace and kissed her. "You're alive. Uh . . . I mean you're not dead. Uh . . . I mean you're here. I thought I'd lost you." He kissed her again, long and hard. "But how?"

"I'll explain later. Right now, we have to stop Duke."

"Stop him from what?"

"From starting the end of the world. He's going to make the final sacrifice."

"He wouldn't do that."

"He doesn't know he's going to. That's why you have to stop him."

Earl belched, and a shred of spirit fell from the corner of his mouth. The wiggling thing hissed in a tiny, tiny voice.

"A god. A god."

Cathy squished the pathetic ectoplasmic speck beneath her sneaker. It expired with a squeal.

Deep red light shone beneath the storeroom door.

"Hurry up. It's almost time!"

"Eyes-ray! Eyes-ray! Eyes-ray!"

Tammy threw her arms wide and gazed into a ceiling alive with writhing tentacles, dripping maws, and shadowy beings of the outer realms straining against the stucco.

"With this offering, I grant thee passage, Frush'ee'aghov! Your time is nigh! Im-sway ee-thay iver-ray of-ay ud-blay at-thay oo-yay ite-may anish-bay ee-thay ite-lay! Eyes-ray! Eyes-ray!"

The scarlet moon cast a crimson glow through the diner windows. The air became the color of blood.

"Now, Chad! Do it now!"

Her disciple didn't hesitate. He drove the kitchen knife deep into Duke's heart. It would have been a fatal blow to the werewolf if the blade had been made of silver. But it wasn't, and all it did was jerk Duke out of his pseudo-death slumber.

One meaty hand grabbed Chad by the throat. The beast tore its way free of Duke's flesh. The towering, hairy wolf howled. His lips drew back in a drooling snarl. He raised a massive clawed hand.

Earl threw open the kitchen door. "Wait, Duke! Don't do it!"

His cries fell on deaf ears. Duke didn't lose his temper often, but when he did, his rage was terrible to behold. After being beaten and stabbed, he reached levels of pissed off even he didn't know he had, and something had to die. Chad was just the most convenient target.

A flash of claws was all it took. Three precise strokes ripped Chad open like a package. His guts spilled to the floor. The stain swallowed the offering with a wailing shriek. Duke tossed aside the corpse as he turned on Tammy. He sprang. An unseen force snatched him from the air and threw him away. He landed beside Earl and Cathy. The jarring blow served to calm him down a touch.

From deep in the earth, the old gods shrieked their rejoicing.

"Goddamn it, Duke," Earl grumbled. "You stupid prick. You just ended the world, you stupid mother—"

Tammy cackled. Her body cracked and warped. Her limbs grew long and spiderlike. Gray streaked her living hair. Her mouth grew to three times its size. Dozens of misshapen teeth poked through bleeding gums.

She spoke with a thousand voices, not one of them human. "The sacrifice shall be made by he who knows not what he does. The Gate shall swing wide, and Frush'ee'aghov the Lesser shall be the first."

Chad's blood collected itself into the black pool. It ate into the floor. A hot wind poured forth. Every glass object in the diner shattered into crystalline powder.

"And he shall open his eye and behold the world and unmake the light. And the old gods shall step upon the world!"

An immense column of slime thrust through the hole. On its tip was a single closed eyelid. Frush'ee'aghov rose higher, smashing his way through the diner's roof.

"Nice going, dipshit," Earl sighed.

And the eye of Frush'ee'aghov slowly began to open.

THIRTY-TWO

It is said by those who study such forbidden knowledge that the old gods existed before time itself, and that they would exist long after eternity has crumbled into oblivion. For such timeless beings, a thousand years is but a blink of the eye. Frush'ee'aghov the Lesser, harbinger of the old gods, was eager to extinguish the light, but time passes slowly for an eternal evil, even an impatient one. The tremendous lids parted to reveal a thin, yellow slit. Dimness spilled over the world like a gray haze covering the universe.

Tammy's thousand voices cackled. She stood before Frush 'ee'aghov, hands raised, chanting in a language older than humanity.

Earl, Duke, and Cathy squatted behind the kitchen counter, happy to be ignored for the moment.

"Goddamn it, Duke," Earl whispered. "You picked a helluva time to lose your temper."

The werewolf growled.

"Watch'a gonna do?" Earl said. "Kill me? Too late for that. You've already killed everybody. And pull that knife out already."

Duke yanked the blade from his chest with a snarl.

Earl couldn't honestly say he was surprised by this turn of events. Life seemed out to screw up his happiness as long as he could remember. And now that he'd found Cathy, hell had to bubble up and claim the world. It made perfect sense, really.

He squeezed her hand.

"I love you."

The words just blurted out. He hadn't said them many times in his hundred years, but there was nothing like the end of the world to put things into perspective. He was glad he'd said it. He'd have been even gladder had she been listening.

A thoughtful expression across her face, Cathy stared at Frush'ee'aghov.

Earl cleared his throat. "Uh, I just wanted you to know that before . . ."

Cathy spoke without taking her eyes off the slimy column. "We can still stop it, Earl. We can send him back before it's too late."

"How?"

"We have to sever his ties to this plane. We have to disrupt the portal and kill Tammy."

"I'll take care of Tammy," Duke said.

He vaulted over the counter and pounced upon the chanting girl. Vicious swiping claws tore her to pieces. She never stopped chanting. Even after her head was ripped from her shoulders, she kept singing the dirge of the old gods. The floor split, and a monstrous tentacle grew behind him. It swatted aside the eight-hundred-pound werewolf with a casual swipe.

Tammy's bits and pieces rose and reassembled themselves. She stopped chanting and strode toward Duke with a gleeful sneer. Her own voice, barely recognizable, boiled to the top of a thousand others. "It's a little late for that, dumbass."

Duke hunched. His eyes reddened with the bloodlust. The man was gone. Only the beast remained, and once it set its mind to killing someone, that person usually wound up dead. Tammy might prove an exception, but the fact she was still alive only enraged him further.

The mutating energies of the old gods threw Tammy's body into chaos. A pair of twisted limbs sprouted from her back. Her neck stretched three feet. Black claws extended from her fingertips. Her skin dripped away to reveal gray, mottled flesh beneath.

Had he an ounce of reason left in him, Duke would have turned and ran, but the wolf wanted blood.

As did Tammy. She crouched on all six and grinned. "You want a piece, little doggie? Come on, and take it."

They sprang. Fang and claw clashed. Flesh ripped. Fur and hair flew. Snarls and growls overwhelmed the shrieks of the old gods. The two monsters spun round and round in a bloody clash. And though Duke gave better than he got, Tammy's wounds healed in moments. His own powers of regeneration weren't holding up nearly as well. Though Earl hadn't thought it possible before, he knew Duke was going to lose this fight.

The vampire moved to join Duke. If he was going to die anyway, might as well go down fighting.

Cathy stopped him. "No, Earl. It won't do any good. She can't die as long as the portal is open."

"How do you know that?"

"It's not important. You've got to trust me."

Earl didn't need much convincing. He already trusted her, and whether she knew what she was talking about or not, he didn't have any better ideas.

"How do we close it?"

"We have to disrupt the interdimensional matrix."

"Matrix?"

"The diner."

"Shit. How are we supposed to destroy this place?"

"We don't have to. We just have to do enough damage to upset the energies holding open the Gate." She pointed to the thick support column. "That right there is the central energy drain. If we destroy it, Frush'ee'aghov will be sent back." She focused on the remnant memories of Gil Wilson. "I think."

"You think, or you know?"

"I know. I think."

The eye of Frush'ee'aghov opened wider. The air turned the consistency of thick coal dust. "Goddamn," Earl sighed, "I hope you're right."

He took her hand and headed for the door. Earl could barely see ten feet through the darkness. He skirted whipping tendrils and smoky crevices. Mere feet from the door, the dark parted to reveal Tammy standing between them and the outside.

"Naughty, naughty. Nobody leaves this party early."

Earl pushed Cathy behind him and switched into full vampire-combat mode. At moments like these he envied werewolves. All he could do was show her his fangs and call upon his scary, undead voice (which wasn't nearly as scary as Tammy's current voices) and try to look intimidating.

"Get out of our fuckin' way!"

"Make me."

Tammy slapped him aside, slashing open his cheek. He stumbled to the wayside.

Cathy swung her bat. The ectoplasmic sphere was one of the half-dozen dimensions brought to the surface of reality by the opened Gate. The spectral bat cracked across Tammy's face. Her long neck swished back and forth like a pendulum. Cathy took a second swing. Tammy caught the blow in one hand. She snatched the ghost up and dangled her over a pit falling through the interdimensional void.

Duke, a streak of black and red fur, crashed into Tammy. The werewolf and the priestess tumbled into the thick fog of unnatural night. Cathy's spirit body fell victim to expectations of gravity. She clung to the pit edge with slipping fingers.

Inhuman shadows hissed and shrieked below. Something slithered around her ankle.

Earl took her arms and yanked her onto solid ground.

She could see the inside of his mouth through the cuts in his face. "Oh my god, are you okay?"

"Just a scratch."

The eye of Frush'ee'aghov buried the world in a heavy twilight. The sounds of Tammy and Duke tearing each other to shreds came from somewhere nearby. Earl's natural night vision allowed him to see, but just barely at that.

"C'mon." He dug his keys out of his pocket and ran for the door.

While the fate of reality was being decided in the dining area, the kitchen was the sight of a lesser struggle. Though much of the interdimensional activity took place in the front, the back was experiencing disturbances of its own. Loretta and Sheriff Kopp stood amidst the madness, rendered helpless by the Dust of Waking Sleep. Warped monstrosities, minor horrors really, crawled on mushy bodies. They were just blobs of flesh with gnashing teeth. All that stood between them and their first meal in ages was one half-faced ghostly Scottish terrier missing his tail.

Napoleon bristled.

All the lesser horrors rolled into one great lump of flesh and two dozen slobbering jaws. Napoleon barked a warning. The hungry thing kept coming.

The humans looked on in frozen terror. They could see the specter, but as the creature was nearly twice Napoleon's size, they didn't hold much hope.

Fearlessly, Napoleon launched himself into his opponent. The creature squealed. It had yet to fully adjust to this reality, and one bite was all it took to deflate it like a hideous, yellow balloon.

Napoleon snorted even as more toothy lumps boiled up through cracks in the floor. The terrier readied himself for battle.

Earl jammed the key in the ignition and started the truck. He flicked on the brights in an effort to see past the hood. It helped a little.

"Where are we going?" Cathy asked.

Earl put the pickup in reverse and backed away, kicking up a cloud of dust and gravel. He ground his way to first gear.

"We're going in."

He fastened his seat belt.

"You sure this is going to work?"

"Pretty sure."

He revved the engine. Steaming fissures cracked the parking lot. The massive tentacles of Frush'ee'aghov thrust through the earth. A writhing wall began sprouting in front of Gil's All Night Diner.

Earl mashed the accelerator while a gap of opportunity remained. The pickup's wheels spun. The truck didn't move. A glance in the rearview mirror showed a gray tendril holding the truck by the tailgate.

"Goddamn it!"

Earl pushed harder, but the pedal was already all the way down. The engine roared. The truck stayed put.

"We're not going to make it!"

Cathy jumped from the cab and hopped in the bed. She brought down her bat on the tentacle's tip. Frush'ee'aghov didn't even notice. Blow after blow after blow accomplished nothing.

"Damn it, let go! Let go!"

Rusted hinges surrendered to opposing forces. The tailgate bent and snapped off. The pickup shot forward, rocketing toward the shrinking hole in the barricade and the unholy temple behind it.

"You're persistent," Tammy mused. "I'll give you that."

Duke was a bloody mess, barely able to keep standing. Organs spilled from a tear in his side. He held them in with one hand, using the other as a third leg. Ragged, wheezing breaths slipped from his throat. His right leg trembled. A jagged bone poked from his left thigh.

Tammy flicked her finger at him. A new cut slashed across

his muzzle. She waved her hand, and five cuts tore into his already thoroughly serrated flesh.

"I'm beyond death now. Beyond the pathetic mortal speck I was, and very soon I'll take my place beside the old gods." She gently cupped his muzzle and raised his head to look into his eyes. "I like you, Duke. You were the one thing I desired I could not have when I was but a child. And even though you could not kill me, you gave it a good try. I respect that. I respect you." A long, red tongue darted from her lips and licked his nose. "That's why I'll offer you this. Join me. As I sit by the new masters of the world, you shall sit by my side. What do you say?"

He spat out a glob of phlegm, vomit, and blood. "Fuck you."

"Have it your way. I could kill you, but I wouldn't dream of denying you the honor of witnessing my ascension to glory."

She slapped him to the floor and turned away. He was of no consequence. She stroked Frush'ee'aghov's slimy mass with loving fingers. The light would forever extinguish soon. In her joy, a flitting thought danced barely in her consciousness. She wondered where Earl and Cathy had gotten to. No doubt crushed beneath Frush'ee'aghov's great body or fallen into hell itself.

A broken headlight cut through the darkness. A battered pickup smashed its way through the front doors. It swerved around a tower of tentacles and collided with the central pillar. The front end wrapped around the cracked column.

Frush'ee'aghov screeched. Tammy felt the Gate narrow. Arcane energies slipped away, but the damage was not enough to stop her. She didn't know how they knew, how they came so close to breaking the matrix. But they had failed, and now she was to become a living goddess. A long, rough chuckle bubbled up within her.

"I cannot be denied!"

The pillar trembled. The pressure of holding up the ceiling and holding open an interdimensional gate were too much to bear. The brick column began to crumble.

"No. This isn't right. This isn't how it's supposed to be."

The central column collapsed, crushing the truck cab, and what was left of the roof fell in. The old gods bellowed as their portal to Earth swung nearly shut. A fraction of their power filtered through the remaining crack. Tammy's body shrank into a vulnerable human shape. Suddenly her will alone anchored Frush'ee'aghov to the world. The strain was immense, almost unbearable, but she need only weather it for a few more moments.

A savage growl issued from behind her. She whirled on the werewolf limping toward her.

"Stay back, or suffer my wrath!"

But there was no wrath to suffer. Even a rudimentary magic required concentration, and all her arcane power was focused on holding open the Gate.

Duke's clawed hand punched through her chest and ripped out her heart. The still beating organ looked tiny in his hand. Tammy stumbled. The old gods poured all their energies into her, but she was dying. If she could just hold on a little longer.

"Stop screwing around, Duke!" Earl called.

Duke squeezed Tammy's heart in his fist. It popped. The priestess of the old gods hissed her last breath.

"Aw, shit."

Frush'ee'aghov sank into the earth. Flailing and thrashing, he fought the irresistible pull. His nearly open eye sucked back through the Gate. A desperate tentacle wrapped around the pickup and dragged it along to hell. Earl and Cathy jumped from the doomed vehicle.

"Damn it!"

Earl tried to save the wreck of twisted steel. The pickup and he had been through a lot together, and he wasn't going to let it go without a fight. The bumper came off in his hands. The automobile bobbed, tipped downward, and sank into the turbulent linoleum sea. It disappeared into the void with a heartrending scrape of warping metal. The dark fog swirled into the bathtub drain of Creation. The many rifts and crevices sealed themselves shut so tight not even the tiniest cracks remained. The old gods shrieked one last defeated cry from their prison.

But it was a distant wail, hardly worth noticing.

The portal closed with a belch and spit out a muffler that came to rest at Earl's feet.

Cathy grabbed him and whirled through the once again seemingly normal diner. There were a few screwups. The tile ran slightly askew. A table stuck through a wall in a mingling of space. The bathroom door had relocated itself several feet from where it once stood, but these were all minor slips in the space-time continuum and easily ignored at the moment.

Napoleon cautiously trotted into the dining area. Cathy knelt and took the dog in her arms. "We did it, boy! We actually did it!"

Duke and Earl glanced up through the gaping lack of roof. The moon and stars were back in place. The thousands of twinkling lights beamed down upon the diner with a blinding brilliance compared to the eternal twilight that had nearly smothered the world. In a hundred years of endless night, Earl had never seen anything as beautiful.

"Thought we cashed in our chips for a second there."

Duke nodded.

Earl stepped in something wet and squishy that had fallen from the leaking gash in Duke's side.

"You alright?"

The werewolf shoved his drooping organs back in place. His canine lips peeled back in a weak smile. "I'll live. How you doin'?"

Earl took a good long look at Cathy. Napoleon licked her face while she laughed. The beauty of the reborn night paled beside her musical giggle.

"Never better."

THIRTY-THREE

Things returned to normal by the end of the week. The citizens of Rockwood were far too accustomed to such happenings to make a big deal out of a little thing like a near apocalypse. The world hadn't ended. Everyone pretended not to notice. Life went on.

There were changes, small shifts in Rockwood's paradigm. The sun shined brighter. The brown grass turned a healthier shade of yellow. A wren was spotted singing sweetly on a diner sign amid a flock of ravens, and a stain of blood on a linoleum floor was finally mopped away for good. And in McAllister Fields two new ghostly guardians stood watch.

Somewhere in the back, two young lovers lay side-by-side, laid to rest in a single ceremony that they might find the happiness in eternity denied them by a tragic coyote attack.

Tammy stood at the graveyard gate. Nothing stood between her and the other side, but she just couldn't step across. It wasn't like there was an invisible wall, yet every time she thought about lifting her leg and crossing, the foot stayed put.

Chad charged the gate. He started from a good way off, but the closer he got, the heavier his steps became. Just before he would have crossed over, he came to a reluctant stop.

"Damn, babe, I thought I had it that time."

Tammy rolled her ectoplasmic eyes. There was no way to break the term of guardianship. They were trapped until somebody died and got buried. Then it was off to whatever waited on the other side for a fallen priestess of the old gods. In the meantime, she could only kill time. She didn't mind the waiting itself, but the company left much to be desired.

Chad tried pushing his fingers past the barrier for the thousandth time and was unsuccessful for the thousandth time. He scratched his head and thought long and hard.

"I think we're stuck."

"Ya think?"

She headed back toward her grave. Chad trailed along.

"So we're, like, dead, right?"

She nodded.

"Bummer." Smiling, he put an arm around her waist. "I just want you to know that I'm not mad about you letting that guy kill me."

"Glad to hear it," she replied through clenched teeth.

His hand slid down to her butt.

Tammy had killed, invoked the forbidden arts, and tried to sacrifice the world for her own gain, but she wondered what she'd done to deserve this.

"Aw, c'mon, baby. We can just make out. We don't have to do anything serious."

Death had not diminished his hormones nor made him any

less annoying. If Chad the ghost was anything like Chad the living, it was just easier to give him a screw and get him off her back.

"Oh, alright," she sighed.

He wrapped her in powerful, yet yielding arms and kissed her. It was strong, passionate, electrifying without being overwhelming. Heat washed through her, and she pushed him away.

"What? Did I do something wrong, babe?"

She took a moment to adjust. Chad had always been a lousy lay when alive. He'd possessed the enthusiasm and the desire. Everything but the talent. He'd always tried, but clumsy hands and a feeble endurance had been his downfall. But ectoplasm was a construction of the soul, and somewhere in Chad hid the soul of a lover.

She kissed him again. The merest touch of his lips made her weak in the knees. She shoved him roughly to the ground. There were worse ways to kill time, she supposed.

He grinned stupidly in a way she found surprisingly charming. Then he opened his mouth and said something stupid to ruin the moment.

"Are we going to do it?"

"Chad."

"Yeah?"

"Shut up."

Deep within the earth, the old gods grumbled. Only Tammy, among the living and the dead, heard.

And she just ignored them.

THIRTY-FOUR

Earl shoved with all his might, but all the unnatural strength of the undead couldn't fit a steamer trunk into the back seat of a used Volvo. He admitted defeat, dropping the trunk to the ground.

"Guess we'll have to tie it to the roof."

"Guess so," Duke went into the diner to borrow some rope.

Earl glared at the stubborn little car. It was a poor replacement for the reliable old pickup Frush'ee'aghov had taken from him.

Cathy sat cross-legged on the hood. He leaned on the bumper beside her and took her hand.

"Do you think he minds me coming along?" she asked.

"Who? Duke? Naw, he's alright with it."

"And what about Napoleon?"

The terrier, complete with a whole head and tail, sniffed around the tires. He raised a leg and took an ectoplasmic whiz.

The ghost pee passed through its target and evaporated upon hitting the gravel. Napoleon proceeded to tour the three remaining targets.

"Duke likes animals."

"Are you sure?"

"Oh yeah."

Earl was reasonably positive. Duke hadn't said anything about it yet. When Earl had mentioned Cathy was going to be traveling with them, he'd just nodded and shrugged. It seemed like a good sort of shrug.

"Y'know, it's funny," she said. "It all came so close to ending."

"Best not to think about it."

"Guess so."

He hopped onto the hood and put an arm around her.

"Cathy, I know we've only known each other a few days and all, and I don't expect you to feel the same way." He fidgeted and twitched. He didn't know why this had been so much easier when he'd thought he was about to die. "And I don't want to scare you or pressure you into saying something you don't really mean or anything, but . . ."

She graced his cheek with a soft peck. "Earl."

"Yeah?"

"I heard you the first time."

She leaned in. Their lips met, and a long minute passed in a tender embrace.

"I love you, too."

She ran her fingers through his thin hair. He smiled crookedly.

Duke and Loretta appeared. Earl tried to wipe the smile off

his face, but it stayed in place. He didn't care. He braced himself for whatever cruel remark Duke might throw at him, but
Duke just shot Earl a look that, try as he might, he couldn't in-
terpret in any bad way.

"Got the rope."

They threw the steamer on the roof and tied it down. Earl
shook his bed to make sure it was in place.

"That'll do."

Loretta awkwardly lowered her ample frame on one
knee so she could pet Napoleon. The interdimensional crisis
had left her and Marshall Kopp with a talent for seeing
ghosts. Though she couldn't pet the dog who had saved
her life, she could stroke the air. It seemed enough for
Napoleon.

"You boys sure you have to go?" Loretta asked. "Wouldn't
mind some help fixing the diner up."

"Thanks for the offer," Earl said, "but it's time we moved
on. Nuthin' personal. Just the way we've been doing things for
so long. Helps to keep us out of trouble. Usually."

Loretta rose with much effort. She dug into her tight shorts
and pulled out a wrinkled fifty-dollar bill.

"That ain't necessary," Duke said. "You already bought us a
car."

She slapped the bill into his hand. "Take it. You boys saved
the world. It's the least I can do."

"You sure keeping the diner open is what you wanna do?"

"Figure a portal to hell should have somebody keeping an
eye on it, and there ain't a whole lot of business opportunities
in Rockwood. All part of the Good Lord's plan. According to

Hector, all it'll take is a few minor renovations to make the diner into a lock instead of a key."

Earl questioned her wisdom, but if she wanted to live atop an interdimensional rift, that was her choice. He did find some comfort knowing the formidable waitress would be guarding the Gate.

He glanced up at the starry sky. "We should get going, Duke. Like to get a few miles under our belt before sunrise."

Loretta slid into Duke's arm. Duke lifted her bulk, calling upon every available ounce of werewolf muscle, and they shared a brief kiss. If planets could make out, Earl supposed that was about what it would look like. Duke set her down.

Loretta adjusted her tangled yellow hair. "You boys feel free to drop by if you're ever passing through again." She threw Duke a wink and a smile and trod back into the diner.

Duke's mouth betrayed a very slight grin.

"You horny bastard," Earl grunted.

They shared a chuckle.

"Give me the keys. I'm driving."

Duke tossed them over the roof. Earl was about to ask Duke to sit in back when he did so without prompting. He whistled, and Napoleon hopped on the seat beside him. The Scottish terrier's tail wagged as Duke went through the motions of scratching Napoleon's chin.

Earl went around and opened the door for Cathy, even though doors meant little to specters. While he was there, he leaned in Duke's window. "Uh, one more thing before we get going. I just wanted to thank you for, uh . . ." He lowered his voice to a whisper so she wouldn't overhear. "Thanks for not killing me."

"Forget it."

Earl climbed behind the wheel and started the car. The Volvo wasn't much to look at, but the engine purred with only the occasional hiccup. A brown police cruiser pulled into the lot as Earl was backing out. Sheriff Kopp stepped out of his vehicle. He tipped his Stetson.

"Where you folks off to?"

Glances were exchanged amidst the passengers. Finally, Cathy spoke up. "I've always wanted to see Las Vegas."

"I went there once. Be sure and catch a magic show while you're there."

The Volvo's occupants all frowned.

"I think we've seen enough magic for a while," Earl replied.

"I guess you're right. Well, have fun anyway." Hands on his belt, he stepped back. "And don't forget to buckle up now. Seat belts save lives."

"Will do."

Earl pulled onto the dirt road alongside the diner. "Vegas, here we come."

"Uh, Earl," Cathy said, "isn't it the other way?"

"She's right," Duke seconded.

"You sure?"

Napoleon yipped.

"Alright, alright."

Cathy by his side, Earl couldn't work up to his standard of irritation. He just smiled, turned the car around, and headed down the road leading out of Rockwood and to wherever the law of Anomalous Phenomena Attraction might lead him. With a vampire, a werewolf, and two ghosts in the car, it was only reasonable to expect a lot of weird shit. Hopefully later rather than sooner. But, for now, there was just Earl, his best friend, his girlfriend, one spectral dog, and a long dirt road heading into a distant horizon and a nice, quiet, normal night.